EROTICA
FIRST PRINTING

10.00

The New Epicurean
&
The Adventures of a School-Boy

The New Epicurean

&

The Adventures of a School-Boy

Two Tales from the
Victorian Underground

Grove Press, Inc.   New York

First Grove Press Edition 1969

First Classics of the Victorian Imagination Edition 1984
First Printing 1984
ISBN: 0-394-54267-3
Library of Congress Catalog Card Number: 84-81072

First Evergreen Edition 1984
First Printing 1984
ISBN: 0-394-62320-7
Library of Congress Catalog Card Number: 84-81072

Printed in the United States of America

GROVE PRESS, INC., 196 West Houston Street,
New York, N.Y. 10014

5 4 3 2 1

The New Epicurean

THE
New Epicurean

OR

THE DELIGHTS OF SEX

FACETIOUSLY AND

PHILOSOPHICALLY CONSIDERED

IN

GRAPHIC LETTERS
ADDRESSED TO YOUNG LADIES OF QUALITY.

Domi maneas paresque nobis
Novem continuas fututiones.
CATULLUS CARMEN XXXII.

A NEW EDITION.

LONDON, 1740 (Reprinted 1875).

[Title page of original edition]

A Note to This Edition

The New Epicurean, a work usually attributed to Captain Edward Sellon, a notorious London rake at the height of the Victorian period, is not a "reprint" of the purported 1740 edition, as its title page would lead one to believe, but an original work, first published in 1865 by William Dugdale, the equally notorious publisher and dealer in erotic books. However, the book was reprinted in 1875 with the identical title and text, except for some unimportant changes in punctuation and the notice "Reprinted 1875."

We learn about Sellon's life from his autobiography, *The Ups and Downs of Life,* a book which no one seems to have seen except Henry Spencer Ashbee (alias Pisanus Fraxi), the famous collector and bibliographer of erotica, compiler of the three-volume bibliography, *Index Librorum Prohibitorum.* Fortunately Ashbee quotes at some length from *The Ups and Downs of Life,* so one still gets a fair idea about the history and character of this curious personality.

It appears that Sellon was born into a moderately wealthy family but lost his father at an early age. As was the custom under those circumstances, he was destined for the army and, according to his own account, at sixteen years of age received a cadetship and soon thereafter was sent with his outfit to India. There he remained for ten years, during which time he became thoroughly acquainted with Hindu life and customs, especially their sexual ones, which seem to have intrigued him greatly from the start. Later he assembled these observations in a now very rare but still important volume, *Annotations on the Sacred Writings of the Hindus, etc.,* London, 1865, which he illustrated himself with a number of drawings.

In India, too, he seems to have taken a liking for very young girls, a passion which remained with him for the rest of his life. *The New Epicurean* is, in fact, essentially a series of fantasies (no doubt partially based on real experiences), involving girls in their mid-teens. The book is written in the form of letters to a number of imaginary young ladies and, in keeping with the facetious imprint "1740," pretends to be in the style of the preceding century.

Young Captain Sellon returned to England and married a girl whom he thought to be very wealthy but who turned out to be of only moderate means. Disappointed in this respect from the outset, Sellon never fully accepted either his wife or the idea of monogamous marriage. The couple actually lived separated for long periods of time, interspersed with longer or shorter periods of reconciliations. At those times, they frequently quarreled, his wife making the most violent scenes of jealousy which, on at least one occasion, led to a serious physical struggle. In the light of these circumstances, it is all the more fascinating that in *The New Epicurean* the author-narrator depicts himself as being rich and married to a beautiful and understanding wife who, not only utterly free of feelings of jealousy, shares in his adventures with a whole bevy of delicious, young girls—a true wish-fulfilling fantasy of the classical textbook type!

In reality, Sellon's life knew of more "downs" than

"ups." He seems always to have been in financial difficulty and unable to resolve his conflict between wanting to lead a respectable upper-middle-class life as a married man and, at the same time, being "footloose and fancy-free" to pursue his other erotic interests, especially those with regard to very young girls. It is, therefore, not too surprising when one learns in the end that, though only forty-eight years of age, Sellon shot himself in April 1866, "at Webb's Hotel, No. 219 and 220 Piccadilly, then kept by Joseph Challis, but since pulled down," as Ashbee comments. Before committing suicide, however, he wrote to a trusted friend telling him of his intention and enclosing the following touching poem, addressed to a woman who, Ashbee says, "was fond of him, and who, when he got into difficulties, wished to keep him":

NO MORE!

No more shall mine arms entwine
Those beauteous charms of thine,
Or the ambrosial nectar sip
Of that delicious coral lip—
      No more.

No more shall those heavenly charms
Fill the vacuum of these arms;
No more embraces, wanton kisses,
Nor life, nor love, Venus blisses—
      No more.

The glance of love, the heaving breast
To my bosom so fondly prest,
The rapturous sigh, the amorous pant,

6 • Two Tales

> I shall look for, long for, want
>   No more.
>
> For I am in the cold earth laid,
> In the tomb of blood I've made.
> Mine eyes are glassy, cold and dim,
> Adieu my love, and think of him
>   No more.
>
> *Vivat Lingam.*
> *Non Resurgam.*

Outside of *The New Epicurean* and *Annotations on the Sacred Writings of the Hindus,* Sellon also wrote *The Monolithic Temples of India,* edited an English translation of the *Ghita-Radhica-Khrishna,* a Sanskrit poem, translated a portion of the *Decameron* by Boccaccio, and did the illustrations for two other classic Victorian erotica, *The Adventures of a School-Boy* and *The New Lady's Tickler.* Aside from this, he also wrote two other erotic short stories. One of these, *The Confessions of a Single Man, as exemplified in the Erotic Adventures of a Gentleman,* was originally meant as a kind of postscript to *The New Epicurean.* Instead, Sellon's publisher, Dugdale, seems to have changed his mind, for he advertised it later as a separate work to be published with "rich engravings" for two guineas. However, the book was never printed and Ashbee claims that the manuscript was in the end stolen and probably destroyed. The other manuscript, entitled *The Delights of Imagination,* which one may presume to have contained more fantasies about pubescent girls, likewise never saw publication.

"Here then," says Ashbee, "is the melancholy career . . .

of a man by no means devoid of talent, and undoubtedly capable of better things." True. But had he left us nothing except this little book, *The New Epicurean,* its delightful fantasies and playful mood would have continued to cheer future generations, just as they had once helped their unhappy author.

The New Epicurean

Gentle Reader,

Before transcribing my correspondence with my fair friends, it is necessary to describe the scene of the amours alluded to in the letters, and also to say a few words regarding the chief actor, myself.

I am a man who, having passed the Rubicon of youth, has arrived at that age when the passions require a more stimulating diet than is to be found in the arms of every painted courtezan.

That I might the better carry out my philosophical design of pleasure without riot and refined voluptuous enjoyment without alloy, and with safety, I became the purchaser of a suburban villa situated in extensive grounds, embosomed in lofty trees, and surrounded with high walls. This villa I altered to suit my taste and had it so contrived that all the windows faced towards the road, except the French ones, which opened on the lawn from a charming room, to which I had ingress from the grounds at the back and which was quite cut off from the rest of the house. To render these grounds more private, high walls extended like wings from either side of the house and joined the outer walls. I thus secured an area of some five acres of woodland which was not overlooked from any quarter, and where everything that took place would be a secret unknown to the servants in the villa.

The grounds I had laid out in the true English style,

with umbrageous walks, alcoves, grottoes, fountains, and every adjunct that could add to their rustic beauty. In the open space, facing the secret apartment before alluded to, was spread out a fine lawn, embossed with beds of the choicest flowers, and in the centre, from a bouquet of maiden's blush roses, appeared a statue of Venus; in white marble at the end of every shady valley was a terminal figure of the god of gardens in his various forms, either bearded like the antique head of the Indian Bacchus, or soft and feminine, as we see the lovely Antinous, or Hermaphroditic—the form of a lovely girl with puerile attributes. In the fountains swam gold and silver fish, whilst rare crystals and spars glittered amidst mother o' pearl at the bottom of the basins.

The gardeners who kept this happy valley in order were only admitted on Mondays and Tuesdays, which days were devoted by me entirely to study, the remaining four being sacred to Venus and love.

This garden had three massive doors in its walls, each fitted with a small lock made for the purpose, and all opened with a gold key which never left my watch guard.

Such were the external arrangements of my Caproe. Now, with a few words on the internal economy of my private *salle d'amour,* and I have done.

This apartment, which was large and lofty, was in its fittings and furniture entirely in Louis Quinze, that is to say, in the latest French mode; the walls were panelled and painted in pale French grey, white and gold, and were rendered less formal by being hung with exquisite paintings by Watteau. Cabinets of buhl and marqueterie lined the sides, each filled with erotic works by the best authors, illustrated with exquisite and exciting prints and charmingly bound. The couches and chairs were of ormolu, covered *en suite* with grey satin, and stuffed with down. The legs of the tables were also gilt, the tops were slabs of marble, which, when not in use for the delicious collations (which were from time to time served up through a trap door in the floor) were covered with rich tapestries. The window curtains were of grey silk and Venetian blinds, painted a pale rose colour, cast a voluptuous shade over the room.

The chimney piece was of marble, large, lofty, and covered with sculpture in relief, representing beautiful naked children of both sexes in every wanton attitude, entwined with grapes and flowers, carved by the hand of a master. The sides and hearth of this elegant fireplace were encrusted with porcelain tiles of rare beauty, representing the Triumph of Venus, and silver dogs were placed on either side to support the wood, according to the style in vogue in the middle of the last century.

To complete the *coup d'œil,* my embroidered suit of garnet velvet, plumed hat, and diamond hilted sword were carelessly flung upon a chair, while the cabinets and sideboards were covered with costly snuff boxes and china. Such were some of the striking features of this delightful chamber. As for the rest of the house, it was furnished like any other respectable domicile of our times.

My establishment consisted of a discreet old housekeeper, who was well paid and not too sharply looked after in the little matters of perquisites and peculations, a bouncing blooming cook, and a sprightly trim housemaid, who were kept in good humour by an occasional half guinea, a holiday, and a chuck under the chin. Beyond these innocent liberties they were not molested. As for the gardeners, they lived out of the house, and being as well paid for their two days' work as if they worked all the week, it followed that they knew their own interests too well to manifest any undue or indiscreet curiosity as to what passed in the grounds when their services were not required.

Having thus given a sketch of the premises, I proceed at once with the letters, only expressing a hope that you, most courteous reader, will quietly lay down the book if it is too strong for your stomach instead of falling foul of

Your humble servant
THE AUTHOR.

To Lesbia

You ask me, most charming Lesbia, to relieve the ennui which your too venerable and too watchful lord causes you to suffer, with his officious attentions, by a recital of some of those scenes which are not visible to the uninitated; and I, having always been your slave, hasten to obey.

You must know then, *chère petite,* that I have certain convenient ladies in my pay, whom I call pointers, forasmuch as they put up the game.

Last Thursday as I lay stretched on a sofa absorbed in that most charming of Diderot's works *La Religieuse,* the silver bell which communicates with the southern gate gave tongue and roused me from my lethargy. I sprang to my feet and wending my way through that avenue of chestnut trees, which you and I, Lesbia, know so well, made direct for the gate. Here the well-known chariot met my eye, and it only required a glance at the smart coachman to show me that jehu was none other than Madame R. herself; and a devilish handsome groom she made, I can assure you.

An almost imperceptible raising of the eyebrows and a gesture with her whip handle towards the interior of the carriage told me all I wanted to know; so first looking up and down the road to see that we were not observed, I whispered, "ten o'clock" and then opened the door. "Come my little darlings," said I to two delicious young creatures, who, coquettishly dressed with the most charming little hats in the world and full petticoats that barely reached their rose coloured garters, sprang, nothing loth, into my arms. The next minute we were all three standing in the garden, the door was locked, and the chariot drove off. The elder of my little pets was a blooming blonde, with soft brown hair that shone like gold, melting eyes of the loveliest blue, and cheeks tinted with the softest blush of the rose, a pert little nose slightly retroussé, carmine lips, and teeth like pearls completed a most delicious face. She was, she said, just thirteen years old. Her companion, a sparkling brunette with dark eyes, raven hair, and a colour that vied with the damask rose, was about twelve. They were charming children, and when I tell you that their limbs were moulded in the most perfect symmetry and that their manners were cultivated, elegant, and gay, I think you will agree with me that Madame R. had catered well.

"Now my little loves," said I, giving each a kiss, "what shall we do first; are you hungry, will you eat?"

This proposal seemed to give great satisfaction, so taking each by the hand I led them to my room; and patties, strawberries and cream, apricots, and champagne disappeared with incredible rapidity. While they were eating, I was exploring; now patting the firm dimpled peach-like bottom of the pretty brunette, now inserting a finger into the pouting hairless cleft of the lovely blonde. The latter was called Blanche and the former Cerise. I was beside myself with rapture, and turning first to one and then to the other, covered them with kisses. The collation finished at last, we all went into the grounds, and having walked them round and shown them everything curious, not forgetting the statue of that most impudent god Priapus, at whose grotesque appearance, with his great prick sticking out, they laughed heartily, I proposed to give them a swing. Of course in putting them in I took care that their lovely little posteriors should bulge out beyond the velvet seat, and as their clothes were short, every time they swung high in the air I had a full expansive view of those white globes, and the tempting rose coloured slits that pouted between them; then, oh! the dear little feet, the fucktious shoes, the racy delectable legs; nothing could be finer. But the sight was too tantalising. We were all heated; I with the exertion of swinging them, they with the wine, so they readily agreed to my proposal to proceed to a retired spot, where was a little lake lined with marble, not more than four feet deep. We were soon naked and sporting in the water; then only was it that I could take in all their loveliness at a glance. The budding small pointed breasts, just beginning to grow; the polished ivory shoulders, the exquisite fall in the back, the tiny waist, the bulging voluptuous hips, the dimpled bottoms, blushing and fresh, the plump thighs and smooth white bellies. In a moment my truncheon stood up hard and firm as a constable's staff. I put it in their hands, I frigged and kissed their fragrant cunnies, I gamahuched them, and then the saucy Cerise, taking my ruby tipped ferrule in her little rosy mouth, began rolling her tongue round it in such a way that I nearly fainted with bliss. At that moment our position was this: I lay stretched on my back on the grass; Blanche sat over me, a leg on either side, with my tongue glued to her rose. Cerise knelt astride of me also, with her posteriors well jutted out towards me, and one of my fingers was inserted in her rosebud. Nor were the hands of the delicious brunette idle; with her right she played with my balls and with the forefinger of her left hand she exquisitely titillated the regions beneath. But human nature could not stand this long; so changing our position I placed Blanche on her hands and knees while Cerise inserted my arrow, covered with saliva from her mouth, into the pretty Blanche. She was tight, but not a virgin, so after a thrust or two I fairly went in up to the hilt. All this while Cerise was tickling me and rubbing her beautiful body against me. Soon Blanche began to spend, and to sigh out, "Oh! oh! dear sir, give it me now! Shoot it into me! Ah! I faint! I die!" and as the warm fluid gushed into her she fell prone on the ground.

When Blanche had a little recovered herself we again plunged into the lake to wash off the dew of love with which we were drenched.

Thus sporting in the water, toying with each other, we whiled away the hours of the afternoon, till tired, at length, we left the lake and dressed ourselves. The sun had long disappeared behind the trees and the shades of evening began to close in. I therefore proposed to adjourn to the villa, where for some time I amused my little friends with bawdy books and prints. But you are not to suppose that my hands were idle, one being under the clothes of each.

Cerise had thrust her hand into my breeches and was manipulating with great industry, which amused me very much; but I soon found out the reason, for presently she said, pouting out her pretty mouth, "You like Blanche better than me!"

"I love you both, my angels," said I, laughing heartily at the little puss's jealousy.

"Ah, it's all very well to laugh," cried Cerise, "but I don't see why I am not to be fucked as well as her!"

"Oh!" I exclaimed, "that's the way the wind blows,

is it!" And drawing the sweet girl to a couch I tossed up her clothes in a moment.

"Quick, quick, Blanche!" cried Cerise, "come and gamahuche the gentleman and make his yard measure stiff before he begins, for you know how tight I am at first."

The little Blanche flung down the book she was looking at, and running up to me placed herself on her knees; then clasping my naked thighs with her milky arms she seized upon the red head of my thyrsus and worked her mouth up and down upon it in the most luscious manner possible. In a few minutes more I could certainly have spent on her tongue had not Cerise, fearful of being baulked, made her leave off. Then guiding the randy prick into her opening rosy little cunny, she began to bound and wriggle and twist until she had worked it well in; then twining her legs around my loins and thrusting her tongue in my mouth she gave way unrestrained to the joys of sensation. I was astonished that so young a creature could be so precocious, but I learnt from Madame R., who had brought her up, that every pains had been taken to excite those passions in this girl since she was seven years of age; first with boys, and subsequently with grown up persons. Blanche I had thought most delicious, but there was a furore in Cerise's fucking which carried you away, as it were, out of yourself.

So great was the delight I experienced with this amorous girl, that I held back as long as possible but she bounded about with such energy that she soon brought down another shower of dew, and all was over. I was glad to hide the diminished head of poor Pego in my white silk breeches, and it being now nearly ten o'clock I rang for chocolate, which soon appeared through the trap door, served up in pretty little porcelain cups with ratafia cakes and bonbons, to which the girls did ample justice. The bell having announced Madame R. at the gate, we went forth hand in hand, having first placed in their pockets a bright new guinea apiece.

Arrived at the gate, I gave her ladyship a pocket book containing twenty pounds, with which she seemed well content.

"Adieu, my dear children," said I; "I hope before long you will pay me another visit."

"Good-bye, sir," cried both the girls in a breath, and the chariot drove off.

Quite tired by this time, I locked the gate, and going round to the front of the villa I knocked and entered, as if I had just come home, retiring soon after to bed to dream over again of the joys of that delightful evening.

To Lais

I am afraid, my pretty Lais, I am in disgrace with you for not writing before, so to excuse my seeming neglect, I will now narrate to you an adventure I have lately had here which will amuse you very much. You may remember, possibly, pretty Mrs. H., the wife of an old prig of a grocer, whom you met here once. Well, she came to see me the other day when, after I had done justice to her charms, which indeed are not to be despised, sitting on my knee and sipping some old Burgundy, for which the fine dame has a great liking, she told me the cause of her visit.

"As you are so generous," she began, "it always gives me great pleasure to oblige you and throw anything in your way that is worthy of the notice of such a true Epicurean. Now I have just received from the country a niece whose father has been long dead and has now lost her mother, so the good people of the place where they lived, to get rid of the orphan, have sent her up to me. This has vexed my good man not a little, as you know he loves his money dearly; not able to get a child for himself, he has no fancy to be saddled with other people's. But I quieted him with the assurance that I would get her a place in a few days. The girl is just seventeen, as beautiful and fresh as an angel and innocent as a baby, so I thought what a nice amusement it would be for you to have her here and enlighten and instruct her. You have, I know, a little cottage fitted up as a dairy; engage her as your dairymaid, buy a cow or two, and the thing is done."

"But," said I, "won't she be afraid to live in the cottage all alone, and if the gardeners should find it out what would they think!"

"Nay, sir," said the tempter, "your honour knows best, but it seems to me that these difficulties can easily be got over. I know an old crone, a simple, poor, humble creature, who would do anything for half a crown and be delighted to live in that cottage. She alone will be seen by the gardeners, and my niece will be kept close during the two days they work in the grounds."

"That will do capitally," said I. "You arrange it all." Accordingly, old mother Jukes and the blooming Phoebe were duly installed. Two alderney cows occupied the cowhouse and the new dairymaid set to work. After two or three days had passed, I went one afternoon to see her milk the cows. She jumped up from her three-legged stool in confusion, and blushing deeply, dropped me a rustic curtsey.

"Well, Phoebe," said I gently, "what do you think of the dairy? Do you think you shall like the place?"

She dropped me another curtsey, and replied, "Yes, an't please ye, sir."

"You find the cottage convenient?" said I.

"Oh! la sir, mighty," cried Phoebe.

"Very good," said I, "now when you have done milking, I will show you the poultry yard and my pet animals, all of which are to be under your care."

As soon as the fair creature had drawn off as much milk as she required, she placed her pails in the dairy and, smoothing down her white apron, attended me. First to the poultry yard, when Phoebe espied the cock treading one of the hens.

"Oh, my," she exclaimed, "that cruel cock; look at him, a pecking, and trampling upon that poor hen, that is just the way they used to go on at feyther's, but I won't let un do it." And she ran forward to drive away the cock.

"Stop, stop, Phoebe," I exclaimed; "do not drive him away, for if the cock does not tread the hen, how are we to have any chickens?"

"Sure, sir, the chickens will come from the eggs, and if he treads upon the poor hen that way, he will break them all in her belly, other while."

"Not at all," said I. "It is true pullets lay eggs, and very good are such eggs for eating, but they will never come to chickens. It is the cocks who make the chickens."

Phoebe opened her large blue eyes very wide at this, and ejaculated, "Mighty!"

"Don't you see, Phoebe, that while he is treading, he is also doing something else?"

"Noa, sir, I doant," said Phoebe demurely.

"If you look at the hen's tail, Phoebe, you will see that it is lifted up and spread open; there, now look; and you will see the cock is putting something in the opening under her tail."

"Oh, la, yes," cried she, blushing as red as a peony; "I see now, well I never."

"You see, Phoebe, you have much to learn; but come to the stable and I will show you something more extraordinary. Where, may I ask, do you suppose foals come from? And kittens, and puppies?"

"Lawk sir, from their mothers, I suppose."

"Yes, but they would not come without they were made; now you shall see what my little stallion pony will do when I let him into the stall of the mare, and some months hence you shall see the foal he has made."

To this Phoebe could only respond, "Mighty."

We went to the stable. The ponies were beautiful little creatures, of a fine cream colour, and pure Pegu breed, sent to me from Burma by a friend.

Like all horses of that colour, their noses, pizzle, etc., were flesh colour, and therefore at once caught the eye. Removing the bar that divided the loose box, I let the stallion pass into the other side. The little mare received him with a neigh of welcome.

"Oh, my," cried Phoebe, "she seems to know him quite nat'ral loike."

The stallion began nibbling at different parts of the mare, who raised her tail, and again neighed. Her lover answered the neigh. Soon he began to scent her sexual beauties, which he caressed with his lips, his enormous yard shot out and banged against his stifle. I pointed it out to Phoebe.

"Oh, good lud! yes, sir, I sees it!" cried she, blushing up very red and trembling all over.

I passed my arm round her taper waist and gently kissing her, whispered, "Now observe what he will do."

Presently the stallion mounted on his hind legs, embracing the mare with the fore ones, his great pizzle began to enter; the mare stood firm and did not kick. He laid his head along her back, nibbling her coat. He moved backwards and forwards. Phoebe trembled and turned red and pale by turns. The mare whinnied with delight, the stallion responded.

"See, Phoebe," said I, "how these lovers enjoy themselves. Mon Dieu! how happy they are!"

"La, sir," cried the girl, "what pleasure can there be in having that great long thing put into her body?"

"The pleasure," said I sententiously, "which nature

gives to those who propagate their kind, and some day my little Phoebe will feel the same pleasure; but look! He has finished, and is out again. See how the female parts of the mare open and shut with spasms of delight. Observe how she cocks her tail—see how she turns her head, as if asking for more. There now, she neighs again."

But Phoebe was not listening; she had seated herself on a truss of hay, and with her eyes fixed on the again stiffening pizzle of the stallion had fallen into a reverie. I guessed what she was thinking about, so seating myself by her side I stole a hand up her clothes. She trembled, but did not resist. I felt her firm plump thighs, I explored higher, I touched her feather; soft and silky as a mouse's skin was the moss in which I entwined my fingers. I opened the lips, heavens! could I believe my senses. She was spending and her shift was quite wet. Whether it was accident or not I cannot say, but she had dropped one of her hands on my lap.

My truncheon had long been stiff as iron; this additional aggravation had such an effect that, with a start, away flew too material buttons and Jack sprang out of his box into her hand. At this she gave a little scream, and snatching away her own hand at the same time, pushed away mine, and jumping up, began smoothing down her rumpled clothes, and with great vehemence exclaiming,

"Oh, la; fie, sir: doantee, doantee. Oh, I'm afeard," etc., etc.

But I was not going to lose such a chance and began to soothe her and talk, until at length we got back to the same position again. I grew more bold, I kissed her eyes and her bosom; I handled her lovely buttocks; I frigged her clitoris—her eyes sparkled; she seized upon that weapon which had at first so frightened her, and the next minute I had flung her back on the hay and was frigging away at her maidenhead, but she made a terrible outcry and struggled most violently. Fortunately, Mrs. Jukes had a convenient attack of deafness, and heard nothing, so that after a good deal of trouble I found myself in possession of the fortress, up to the hilt. Once in, I knew well how to plant my touches, and ere long a soft languor pervaded all her limbs, pleasure succeeded pain. She no longer repulsed me, but sobbing on my shoulder, stopped now and then to kiss my cheek.

Her climax came at length and then she threw all modesty aside, entwined her lovely legs around my back, twisted, wriggled, bit, pinched, and kissing me with ardour, seemed to wake up to the new life she had found.

Thrice we renewed the seraphic joys; and then and not till then did I leave her to her poultry yard and her dairy.

She is still with me; an adept in the wiles of love; not the least jealous, but very useful to me in all the other little affairs which I have on hand. As for Mrs. H., I gave her fifty guineas for her niece's maidenhead; and although I have bought many much dearer, I never enjoyed it as I did with Phoebe.

So now good night, and if you can sleep without a lover after such a recital, it is more than I can; so I shall seek the arms of this unsophisticated country lass to allay the fires that recording this narrative has lit up in my veins.

To Sappho

You complain, my sweet girl, that it is long since you heard from me, and remind me that I, of all men, am the only one who could ever give you delight. In reply to your complaint, I must assure you that had there been anything to relate which would have been likely to interest my young philosopher I should have written, but I know too well that ordinary love affairs between men and women do not much amuse you and that the loves of girls for each other are more to your taste. By your other remark I am much flattered; and if you can frame some excuse to your aunt for leaving home and will come here, I think I can show you how to pass an agreeable afternoon. In the interim I will detail an adventure which I met with the other day, and I think will vastly please your fancy.

I was strolling out in one of those thick woods which abound in this neighbourhood when in a secluded dell I espied two young ladies seated very lovingly together, engaged in earnest conversation. They were so absorbed in their discourse that I found no difficulty in approaching softly to within a yard of the spot and, concealing myself in a thicket, sat down on the turf to listen to them.

The elder of the two was a fine handsome woman of about five or six and twenty, with lustrous dark eyes, black hair, an aquiline nose, and noble figure, yet rather too masculine looking to be altogether pleasing. Her companion was a lovely girl of sixteen, a most exquisite face of a perfect oval, laughing blue eyes shaded with long black lashes, and a profusion of the most beautiful hair of a light auburn which wantoned in the breeze in a hundred lovelocks, forming a most charming picture; her figure was exquisitely rounded in all the witchery of early girlhood, and its undulations raised certain strong desires in my heart to be better acquainted with its beauties.

I now set myself to listen to their conversation.

"I assure you," the dark-eyed woman was saying, "there is nothing in it; these men are the most selfish creatures in the world; and besides what pleasure, think you, can they give us that we do not have already without their aid?"

"Well, dear friend," laughed the girl, in a sweet silvery voice, "I am sure you talk very sensibly, but yet there must be something in the joys of love, if we are to believe the poets, who have so often made it their theme; besides, I do not mind telling you that I know a little more about the subject than you may suppose."

"Mon Dieu," ejaculated the dark beauty, who I now began to think was a Frenchwoman, especially as I had already noticed a slight foreign accent in her voice; "Mon Dieu" (and she turned pale) "how is it possible you should know anything of love at your age?"

"Shall I tell you?" replied the young girl.

"Ah! yes, yes; tell me, ma chère."

"Well then, dear; you know young Mrs. Leslie?"

"Certainly."

"She was a former school-fellow of mine; and a month or two after her honeymoon, I went on a visit to that pretty country seat of her husband's, Harpsdeen Court, in Bedfordshire. While there she not only told me all about the secret joys of matrimony, but permitted me to witness her bliss."

"To witness it? Incredible!"

"'Tis a fact, I do assure you; shall I tell you what I saw, and how I saw it?"

"Oh yes, *ma petite,* I do not mind what you may have seen, I was only afraid one of these perfidious men had captivated your poor little heart; as it was a mere girlish frolic, it will amuse me very much to hear all about it."

The young girl, first giving her friend a sweet kiss, which I envied, thus began:

"My friend Clara Leslie, though not strictly handsome, has a pleasing amiable face, but nature, you know, is full of compensations, as her husband found out to his great satisfaction. She has a shape that vied with the Venus de Medici, the most lovely figure you ever beheld. When quite a girl at school, she could show a leg that any woman might envy, but now at twenty years of age she surpassed the finest statue I ever saw. I will not trouble you with a recapitulation of all that passed on her wedding night, and subsequently up to my arrival at Harpsdeen, because you, my sweet friend, doubtless know all that occurs on such occasions, but will confine myself to what I saw. She proposed to me to sleep in a room adjoining theirs, divided only by a thin oaken wainscot in which one of the knots in the wood could be taken out at pleasure and thus command a full view of the nuptial couch. Clara told me she would place a pair of wax lights on a table near the bed, and out of regard to me would so manage matters that I should see all that passed between her and her handsome husband, the squire. Accordingly, we all went to bed about ten o'clock one night, and I having undressed and wrapped myself in my *robe de chambre,* placed myself on an ottoman over against the panel. Assisted by her husband, Clara was soon reduced to a state of nature and stood naked like a beautiful Eve, with her lovely hair meandering down her alabaster back and shoulders.

" 'Charles, dear,' said my sweet friend, 'do you lie on the foot of the bed and let me mount you, à la St. George, you call it, I believe. I do so love that position.'

"He kissed her tenderly, and being now himself naked, flung himself back on the foot of the bed.

"Then, dearest Maria, I saw, for the first time, that wondrous ivory staff with its ruby-crested head, rising from a nest of glossy black curls. Having waited a moment to give me an opportunity of seeing it, she pressed her face in his lap and took the head of his noble toy in her mouth; then after moistening it for a few seconds, she mounted astride him, displaying to my delighted gaze her large beautiful dimpled bottom and lily white thighs, between which I could clearly discern the mark of her sex; then grasping his wand in her little hand, she guided it in and immediately began to move up and down *à la postillon.*

"He clasped those white hemispheres with his hands, he squeezed them together, he held them open, he thrust his finger into the nether rosebud, he kissed her breasts, while mutual sighs of delight escaped the fond pair. As for me, I was so excited as to be almost beside myself, and felt almost suffocated. At length, I sought relief in the schoolgirl's substitute and used my finger for want of something better. Though this was but a poor expedient, it relieved the burning heat and caused a flow of love's dew, which allayed the itching desire which had taken possession of me. Meantime, Clara's climax and Charlie's came simultaneously and they lay panting in each other's arms. In a very short time, however, he was again ready for action, and making Clara kneel upon the bed he stood behind, and again the amorous encounter was renewed. Four times in various attitudes did he repeat the play, and then putting out the candles they retired to rest.

"As for me, I could scarcely sleep at all; all night I was tossing about, trying in vain with my finger to procure myself that satisfaction which I had seen her enjoy.

"Now my dear Marie, inveigh as much as you please against love; for my part the sooner some nice young fellow takes a fancy to me the better I shall like it."

"My dearest child," cried the dark beauty, "I dare say it is very true that your friend has made a very excellent match and is quite happy in her husband, but what I want to impress upon you is, that for one such marriage as that, there are ten wretched ones. Besides, I will, if you like, soon demonstrate to you that there is more pleasure to be derived from the love of woman for woman than any that the male can give. We are all alone here in this lovely glen; let me show you how I will make love."

"You!" cried the young girl. "What? Are you going then to make love to me?"

"To yourself, my pet," whispered hoarsely the salacious woman, as her dark eyes gleamed and her hand passed up the clothes of her companion.

"Oh; but," said the younger, "this is very droll, good heaven, what are you about! Really, Marie, I am surprised at you."

"Do not be surprised any longer then, my little angel," cried her friend. "Give me your hand," and she passed it up her own clothes. "Now, I will show you how to touch that little secret part. It is not by putting the finger within that the pleasure is to be gained, but by rubbing it at the top, just at the entrance; there it is that nature has placed a nerve called by doctors the clitoris, and it is this nerve which is the chief seat of bliss in our sex." All this while the libidinous creature was manipulating with skill.

The colour came and went in the cheeks of her beauteous companion, who faintly sighed out, "Ah, Marie, what are you doing? Oh, joy; oh blissful sensation! Ah, is it possible—oh—oh—ur—r—r—r." She could no longer articulate.

The tribade saw her chance, and waited no longer; so throwing up the clothes of the young girl, she flew upon her like a panther, and forcing her face between the thighs of her friend, gamahuched her with inconceivable frenzy. Then, not satisfied with this, she pulled up her own clothes and straddled over the young girl, presenting her really symmetrically formed posteriors close to her face, nearly sitting down upon it in her eagerness to feel the touch of the young girl's tongue. Nor had she to wait long; wrought up to the last pitch of lascivious extasy, her friend would have done anything she required, and now gamahuched her to her heart's desire.

I continued to watch these tribades for some time, revolving in my mind how I could get possession of the young one, for whom I had conceived a most ardent longing.

Suddenly it occurred to me that, as they were strangers in the neighbourhood, it was not likely they had walked, and that possibly, on the outskirts of the wood, I should find a coach waiting for them.

Full of designs upon the pretty young creature, I left the amorous pair to their amusement and soon reached the margin of the road. Here, ere long, I espied a coach and six with servants in rich liveries, and approaching nearer saw from the coronet on the door that it belonged to some person of quality. As I came up I accosted one of the lacqueys, and tossing him a crown, asked whose carriage it was.

"His Grace the Duke of G—'s, your honour," said the man, touching his hat respectfully as he glanced at my embroidered coat, sword and diamond buckles, and pocketing the crown.

"Then you are waiting, I presume, for the two ladies in the wood?" said I.

"Yes, sir," replied the lacquey; and being a talkative, indiscreet person, he added, "Lady Cecilia Clairville, his Grace's daughter, your honour, and Madame La Conte, her governess."

"Ah, indeed!" said I, with as indifferent a manner as I could assume, and passed on.

At a turn of the road, I again dived into the wood and soon reached my own demesne.

"A very pretty affair, truly," said I to myself as I took a glass of wine. Madame La Conte, engaged by the duke to complete the education of his daughter, takes advantage of her position to corrupt her, and by making her a tribade renders her wretched for life; for let me tell you, Sappho, there is no more certain road to ill health, loss of beauty, pleasure, and all the zest of life, than this horrid lust for the wrong sex.

"Very well, Madame La Conte," I soliloquised, "I shall turn this discovery to account, you may depend"; and with that resolve I went to bed.

Next morning I sent a billet in French by a trusty messenger to his grace's mansion in Cavendish Square. It was as follows:

> Madame, to all that passed between you and the lady Cecilia in the wood yesterday I was a witness. I am a man of position, and if you do not wish me to call upon the duke and acquaint him with your nefarious proceedings, you will come tomorrow afternoon at three o'clock to the big oak at the east end of the same wood, in a hackney coach, which you will alight from at the west side. To avoid discovery you had better both be masked.
> Yours, as you behave yourself,
> ARGUS.

Punctual to the appointment I had made, I placed myself beneath the shade of the oak, and as there was no saying what might happen, or what ambush this devil of a Frenchwoman might lay for me, I, besides my sword, put in my pocket a brace of loaded pistols. Soon the fair creatures approached, hand in hand. I raised my hat to the young girl, but as for madame, I merely honoured her with a contemptuous stare.

"Do not be alarmed, Lady Cecilia," said I; "you are with a man of honour, who will do you no harm. As for you, madame, you may make a friend or an enemy of me, which you will."

"Really, monsieur," said the governess, "your conduct in this affair is so singular that I know not what to think; but let me tell you, sir, that if you have any improper designs in inveigling us to this place, I shall know how to be avenged."

"Doubtless, doubtless, madame; I know the French well and have well prepared for all contingencies. But allow me, ladies, to offer each an arm, and do me the honour to walk a little further into the wood."

The alacrity with which the wily Frenchwoman complied told me at once what I had to expect.

She had resolved to assassinate me. Having made up my mind how I should act, I allowed her to lead me which way she pleased, keeping, however, a sharp look out on all sides as we strolled along. I was about to enter upon the subject of their coming, when suddenly three masked highwaymen sprang out, and demanding, "Your money or your life," levelled their horse pistols at us. The ladies screamed; I shook them both off, and as one of the scoundrels sent a bullet through my wig, I drew my pistols from my pocket and shot him dead; his companions then both fired, one of the bullets grazed my shoulder, but the other, curious enough, pierced the head of Madame La Conte, who, casting a glance full of fury upon me and clenching her hands, fell back a corpse.

The remaining rascals turned to flee; but before they could escape I brought down a second, and attacking the third with my sword, soon passed it through his lungs.

The enemy being now utterly defeated, I turned towards the lovely Lady Cecilia, who had fainted; and raising her light form in my arms, bore her off to the spot where the coach had been left. But it was gone. The jarvey, doubtless hearing the firing and anxious to save his skin, had driven away. My resolution was taken in a moment. So carrying my fair burthen to the nearest gate that opened into my grounds, I bore her to my secret chamber, and having fetched old Jukes and Phoebe to her assistance, with strict orders not to tell her where she was but to pay her all needful attention, I saddled a swift horse and rode off to the nearest town, one of the magistrates there being an old friend.

He was much pleased to see me, but wondered at my being covered with dust and at my sudden arrival. I told him a most dreadful affair had happened; that returning home, I heard cries for assistance in the wood, and found three ruffians robbing and ill using some ladies; that they had fired at and wounded me and killed one of the ladies; as for the other she escaped.

That in the end I had succeeded in dispatching the rascals, more in consequence of their want of skill in the use of their weapons than from any extraordinary valour on my part, and finally requesting him to give orders to have the bodies removed with a view to a coroner's inquest. All which he promised to do; and in spite of his earnest request that I should stay and drink a bottle of wine, I made my excuses and returned home.

I found my fair guest much better, and having consoled her as well as I could for the loss of Madame La Conte, I then gradually unfolded to her all the wickedness of that vile woman, and after delicately touching upon the scene in the wood the day before, I told her I had been a witness of it all and heard all the conversation.

At this denouement, Lady Cecilia covered her face with her hands to hide her blushes; and when I enquired whether Madame La Conte had shown her my letter, she said she knew madame had received a letter, which was very unpleasant, which she tore up and burnt in a great rage, but as to its contents she was ignorant.

This was very satisfactory news for me, as my handwriting might have been recognized. So turning to the young girl with a cheerful countenance, said, laughingly,

"Well, my dear young friend, all is well that ends well; now let us make plans for the future. In the first place, it seems to me that you are formed for the joys of love. It is true I am not quite so young a lover as you might desire; but I am more fit for amorous combats than many younger men. I am rich, and though not absolutely a man of rank I am a scion of a noble house. What do you say? I know your secret. I have already seen all your charms; shall we make a match of it? Will you marry me?"

"Indeed, sir," said the dear girl, "your gallantry in attacking those ruffians and defending my honour would alone have been sufficient to win my heart; but as my father, the duke, has designs of wedding me to a man older than himself, an old creature whom I detest, I deem this meeting with you a most fortunate one and will accept your offer with the same ingenuous frankness with which you have made it. You say, truly, that you have already viewed my person with pleasure; take it, dear sir, and do what you please with me. I am yours forever."

I was quite enraptured with this decision, and it being determined that the duke should be written to in the morning and informed that his daughter, entertaining an insuperable objection to the match he had in store for her, had eloped with the man of her choice.

This affair settled, and Phoebe with many sly glances having made up a bed on one of the sofas, I shut the windows and hastened to undress my future bride. She was exquisitely formed, with the most lovely breasts in the world; and as for her bottom and thighs, nothing could be finer.

We were soon in bed, and all that her finger and the wanton tongue of madame had left of her maidenhead, I soon possessed myself of. Dawn found us still in dalliance; but at length, being both quite fatigued, with a last sweet kiss we fell asleep. The next day we were to be privately married by license.

So now, my dear Sappho, I must conclude this long letter by saying to you, "Do thou go and do likewise."

To Julia

Your letter, giving me an account of your adventure with the Marquis at Ranelagh Gardens, diverted me vastly. Meantime, I have not been idle.

Since you were last here, I have colonised one corner of my grounds. A discreet old creature called Jukes, has been placed in charge of that pretty cottage covered with roses and jasmine which you admired so much; and in the dairy she is assisted by the freshest and most charming of country girls. Positively you must come and pay me a visit, if only for the pleasure you will experience in the sight of Phoebe's perfections; but this is a digression and I know you hate digressions; therefore to proceed.

Phoebe and I, you must know, quite understood each other, but she is so pretty, brisk, loving and lively, and time, place and opportunity so frequently present themselves, that I have nearly killed myself with the luscious fatigue, and having fucked her in every imaginable attitude, having gamahuched her and been gamahuched in return, I at length cloyed and began to look out for some new stimulant; but alas, Madame R. did not call; I saw nothing of Mrs. H. To write to them was not in accordance with my usual prudence. What was to be done? I was in despair. At this juncture, that dear old Jukes came to my aid, though very innocently, as I believe. With many curtseys and "Hope your honour's worship won't be offended at my making so bold," etc., she told me that she would be greatly beholden if I would allow her to have a little orphan grandchild of hers to live with her and Phoebe in the cottage.

She told me that her little girl was a sweet pretty creature, ten years of age, and as she knew that I liked to amuse myself with children sometimes (?), poor innocent soul, she thought I might like to have her.

I at once consented, and in a few days arrived one of the sweetest flowers that ever blushed unseen in the woods of Hampshire. I was charmed, and lost no time in providing suitable clothes for the little pet, and, with the aid of Phoebe, her frocks were so contrived that they only reached her knees. This, you will readily understand, was for the purpose of giving me facilities for seeing her young beauties without doing anything that might alarm her young innocence. We soon became great friends, and she took at once to Phoebe, the swing, the goldfish, strawberries and cream, the rambles in the woods, and above all her handsome new clothes; all combined to render little Chloe as happy as a princess; while her old granddam would follow her about exclaiming, "Lawk a mercy! well I never!" and so on.

In the course of a few days, our young rustic had quite rubbed off her first shyness, would run in and out of my room, sit on my knee, hide my snuff box, kiss me of her own accord, and play all sorts of innocent tricks, like other children, in swinging, climbing up trees, and tumbling about on the grass; the little puss not merely showing her legs but everything else besides.

At first Mrs. Jukes tried to stop it, and told her it was rude to behave so before the gentleman, but I begged she would take no notice in future as I did not mind it and liked to see the little girl unrestrained and happy.

Now old Jukes always went to bed at sunset; I therefore arranged with Phoebe that after the old crone was gone to rest she should wash Chloe all over every night before putting her to bed; and that it might be done properly, I used to go and witness the operation, for it gave me a pleasureable sensation to see the child naked when Phoebe was present.

Phoebe was a clever girl and did not require much telling, so that none of the most secret charms of my little Venus were concealed from my lascivious gaze.

At one moment Phoebe would lay Chloe across her lap, giving me a full view of her little dimpled bum, holding open those white globes and exposing everything beneath. Then she would lay the girl on her back and spread out her thighs, as if to dry them with the towel. In fact, she put her into almost every wanton attitude into which she had seen me place myself. The little innocent girl, meanwhile, seemed to think this washing process capital fun, and would run and skip naked about the room in the exuberance of her animal spirits.

In this amusement I found all the excitement I desired, and should perhaps have been content with viewing her beauties without attacking her innocence but for a circumstance that occurred.

One evening, after the usual performance of washing, skipping about, etc., the little saucebox came and jumped on my knees, putting a leg on either side of them, and began courting a romp. Had I been a saint, whereas you know I am but a sinner, I could not have resisted such an attack on my virtue as this.

Only imagine, my dear Julia, this graceful lovely creature in all the bloom of early girlhood, stark naked except her stockings, her beautiful brown hair flowing over her exquisite shoulders; imagine her position, and how near she had placed herself to the fire and then, say, can you blame me?

In fine, I slid my hand down and released that poor stiff prisoner, who for the last half hour had nearly burst open his prison; as a natural consequence he slid along between her thighs and his crested head appeared (as I could see by the reflection in an old mirror) impudently showing his face, between her buttocks on the rear side. She would perhaps have noticed it, were it not that my finger had long been busy in her little slit already "tickling," she called it, and laughed heartily, tickling me under the arms in return.

Suddenly, as if a thought struck her, she said, "Do you know that—"

She paused. Never did man wait with more exemplary patience.

"That—that—"

Another pause.

"That I saw—"

Pause again.

"The cock—"

Here Phoebe tried to stop her, but she squeezed her interrupter's two cheeks so that she could not speak and hurriedly concluded, "Making chickens—there."

This was too much for my gravity, and I was convulsed with laughter; when I had a little recovered, I asked, "And how does the cock do that, my dear?"

"Why," said Chloe, with the most artless manner in the world, "he tickles the hen, and when she lays eggs they come to chickens."

"Tickles her! I do not understand," said I.

"But he does," insisted the little girl.

"But the cock has no fingers; how can he tickle?"

"Why," cried Chloe triumphantly, "he has got a finger, and a long one too, and I saw it shoot from under his tail when he was treading the hen, and he tickled her, just as you are tickling me now, but putting it right into her body. Now, am I not right in saying the cock makes chickens by tickling the hen?"

"Well reasoned, my little logician," cried I, really pleased with her wit. "I see, though you have lived in the country, you are no fool, and I will tell you something which little girls are always very curious about but which their mothers and grannies will never tell them anything of. But first tell me why you thought the cock tickling the hen made the chickens."

"Why, because Phoebe told me, to be sure."

"Oh, ho!" said I, laughing. "You told her, Phoebe, did you?"

Poor Phoebe looked frightened out of her wits.

"I hope you will forgive me, sir, but Chloe did worrit so, and keep all on about that ere beast of a cock that at last I up and told her."

"God bless you, my dear girl. What if you did? There is no harm in that, I hope. There can never be anything wrong in what is natural."

Then turning to Chloe, whose little cunny I had not let go of all this while, "Would you like to know, my dear, where the babies come from and how they are made?"

"Oh, yes; that I just should," exclaimed Chloe, hugging and kissing me.

"Very well; now you know, I suppose, that you are not made exactly like a little boy, do you not?"

"Yes, I know that down here, you mean," and she pointed to where my finger was still tickling.

"Just so. But did you ever, by chance, happen to see a man?"

"Never."

"And you would like to?"

"Of all things."

"There then!" cried I, lifting her up and allowing the rampant yard to spring up against my belly.

"Oh, the funny thing!" said Chloe, then taking hold of it, "how hot it is. That is what I have felt against my bottom these last ten minutes and could not think what it was; but what has that to do with making babies?"

"I will show you," said I, "but I cannot promise you that I shall make one, as I am too old for that, but it is by doing what I am going to do to Phoebe that children are begotten."

"Oh, I see!" cried the little girl, clapping her hands, "you are going to serve Phoebe as I saw the stallion serve the mare today. That will be capital fun."

"Serve the mare," I ejaculated, glancing over my shoulder at Phoebe. "How's this?"

"Well, the truth is, sir," said the conscious girl, "ever since your honour showed me that trick I have often gone to see them do it, and I was watching them today when this little scapegrace came running into the stable. So I was obliged to tell her all about it, as I did about the chickens."

"Well," said I, "if she has seen that, I see no harm in her seeing the other; so pull up your clothes, my dearest creature."

In a moment Phoebe had tucked up her petticoats, and kneeling on the truckle bed and jutting her white posteriors well out, presented a full view of all her charms.

"Oh, my," cried Chloe, "why Phoebe, you have got hair growing on your—"

She stopped, and with a charming blush, hid her face in my bosom.

"And so will you have, my little maid," I whispered, "when you are as old as she is; but now observe what I am going to do, and mind you tickle me underneath all the while."

This she did in the most delightful manner, occasionally laughing to see Phoebe wriggling about. As soon as all was over, I sent Phoebe to my room for some refreshments and wine, and while she was gone I gamahuched the lovely little Chloe, which operation, coming as it did after all the frigging she had undergone, roused at once her dormant passions into precocious energy. With eagerness she seized my again erect wand, and putting it into her little mouth, worked it up and down so that, just as Phoebe returned, I sent a spirting shower over her tongue while her virgin dew drenched my own.

"Oh, my! how salty it is," sputtered the little girl, spitting and making a wry face.

"And is it that stuff, sir, that makes the babies?"

"One drop of it, my dear, is sufficient to make a little girl as pretty as you."

"Or a little boy?"

"Yes, or a little boy."

After supper, Chloe, who said she was not at all sleepy, wanted Phoebe and me to perform again, but I told her that was quite enough for one night and that she was on no account to say anything of what she had seen to her granddam.

Now I think my dear Julia will say I have related a most interesting adventure; but really, I wish you would come and stay a few days and share in our sports. I shall confidently expect to see you before long.

To Euphrosyne

Your pretty cousin Sappho will doubtless have told you the startling news, that I am—what do you think?—married! It is true, however, and a very charming little creature my wife is, I can tell you.

Quite free from all those silly notions of propriety and jealousy, her chief delight is to make me happy, not only by giving up to me her own pretty person but by throwing in my way any chance that may occur when there is any new face that pleases me.

With this view, she proposed to me that we should adopt the two little daughters of a cousin of hers who, being poor, accepted a situation in the East India Company's service, and having subsequently contracted in the East an imprudent marriage, these children were the fruits of it. Their mother being dead, he sent them home to be educated; and by a singular chance they were placed at the school of Mrs. J., who you know is a tenant of mine and occupies that house near this place which I offered to your papa some years ago.

Of course, after my marriage I presented Cecilia to my household as their mistress, no object being gained by keeping it a secret; and there is a great convenience in this, as whatever they may have thought before about the secret chamber and grounds, as my wife is now with me it silences scandal at once. Now I will go on to relate to you the acquisition this plan of my wife's has produced.

We drove over to Mrs. J., with whom I was always a favourite; and with reason, as more than once when she was a little straitened for her rent I have sent her a receipt for the money without ever receiving it.

She is the widow of a naval officer, and though over five and thirty years of age, has still the remains of considerable personal attractions.

She was at home and delighted with our visit. So we opened the object of it.

"My dear Mrs. J.," began Lady Cecilia with the smile of a seraph, "I have persuaded Sir Charles to allow me to adopt my poor cousin's little girls, and I now intend to take the entire charge of these young ladies."

Then observing Mrs. J. began to look very thoughtful, she quickly added, "But do not misunderstand me. I mean not to remove them from your excellent supervision; their education must of course proceed as usual. All I want is permission to break through one of your rules and ask you to let them come and pass a few days with us sometimes, instead of coming for the regular holidays."

"I am sure," cried Mrs. J., whose countenance had quite cleared up during this speech, "I shall be vastly pleased to oblige your ladyship in any way in my power. Pray arrange it just as you like."

"And if," added I, "my dear Mrs. J., you will yourself occasionally favour us with your company and bring any of your young ladies with you, we shall both, I am sure, be enchanted. You know I have some pretty grounds to which I do not admit everybody, but your name will be an 'open sesame' at all times."

"Oh, Sir Charles," cried the good lady with a conscious blush (which showed she knew those precincts well), "you are too good, I am sure. But really, to tell you the truth, I was quite frightened when I saw your carriage drive up the avenue, as I remembered there are two quarters' rent in arrear; indeed, I am afraid you find me a sorry tenant."

"I would not change you, my dear madam, for all the best tenants in the world. But see, I anticipated your fears, well knowing the sensibility of your nature and your honourable sentiments; here is the receipt, and as for the money, pray accept it to procure any little article of jewellery you may require."

Mrs. J. glanced furtively at my wife before she replied; but seeing nothing in that sweet face but the most amiable and charming smile she said at once, "Oh, Sir Charles! how very considerate and kind you are; always the same noble gentleman, madam," she continued, turning to Lady Cecilia, "so kind, so generous."

"Then it is all settled," said Cecilia; "and remember to bring some of the prettiest of your young ladies. You know Sir Charles loves a good romp with young girls, and I am not at all jealous."

"Oh, my lady, I can see you are a sweet creature, and I am delighted Sir Charles has made such a happy choice. I will bring two or three of my girls with your dear little cousins; but will you not see them before you go?"

"Oh, yes, certainly; send for them, I beg."

Mrs. J. rang the bell, and presently appeared two of the most lovely, blooming children I had ever seen. Augusta and Agnes they were called, one nine and the other eleven years old. They had the sweetest and most innocent countenances in the world, and their manners did ample justice to Mrs. J.'s training. I took one on each knee, and as I kissed their rosy cheeks I felt over their muslin frocks that they had each nice, firm, plump little bottoms, with which I hoped ere long to be better acquainted.

Mrs. J. saw the movement, and smiled archly. Then catching Cecilia's eye, "A sad man! a sad rake! is he not, my lady?"

"Oh, indeed he is!" cried Cecilia, laughing; "and if I mistake not, you and I know all about it, *n'est-ce pas?*"

Mrs. J. blushed scarlet, but seeing that the remark was mere playful badinage and not malicious, she soon recovered her presence of mind. After a merry chat with the little girls, the tip of a guinea a piece, and the promise of new dolls, we took our leave.

As soon as we were in the carriage my wife gave me a tap with her fan, saying, "Positively, Charles, you are incorrigible; I do verily believe that Mrs. J. is an old flame of yours."

"Of course she is, my love; and a deuced fine woman she was, I can assure you; a little stale now, perhaps, but a most useful person, and so prudent. Whenever she has had any orphan girls, or girls whose friends did not pay well or punctually, if they were pretty (and she will not take ugly ones), she has always brought them to me; and in this way for five guineas I have bought many a little maidenhead of her. Yet so cleverly has she managed matters that nothing unpleasant has ever arisen out of these affairs. There was one case, indeed, which I had almost forgotten, which was rather awkward, as the fool of a guardian thought proper to take offence upon his ward complaining to him; and he came down here in a towering passion with Frank Firebrace of the Guards. He waited in the wood and sent the captain to me with a cartel.

"I was not the man to refuse such a summons, but told him he must wait till I also sent for a friend.

"I knew where an old chum of mine was to be found

and posted off a messenger for him. On his arrival we started to the place of rendezvous, and there, on that deep dell which you admire so much, I was under the disagreeable necessity of killing the guardian of the little girl while O'Brien made an end of poor Firebrace. I was vexed with him, I remember, for this, but he quieted me with, 'Don't you see, my dear fellow, in a delicate affair like this, there is nothing like securing silence; and sure dead men tell no tales, at all, at all.' As for the girl, we smuggled her out of the country and locked her up in a convent. Egad, it was a deuced unpleasant business and made poor Mrs. J. very much afraid of Bridewell, at the time."

"Oh! dear Charles," said Cecilia, "how charmingly wicked you are, and vastly cool too you seem to speak of it. You naughty man, I do believe you ravished the girl."

"Oh, yes," said I, "it was doubtless what the law called a rape."

"And what had Mrs. J. to do with it?"

"Ah, she brought the girl to me and held her down while I deflowered her. You see the girl was a little Puritan whom we had, in vain, tried to break in; but her modesty was superior to either menaces or presents. Unfortunately, she was very beautiful, and only thirteen, and the opposition made me mad for her. But do not let us speak of it any more; it was one of those contretemps which occasionally mar the uniform career of a man of pleasure."

"Really, Charles, you quite frighten me with your coolness. But never mind, you dear man, I love you with all my heart and shall never think very harshly of your little peccadilloes."

The following Thursday brought Mrs. J., the two young cousins, and three other young ladies about whom it will be necessary to say a few words.

Miss Marshall was a poor Irish girl from the county of Kerry, whose unnatural father, a naval officer, having placed her three years before with Mrs. J., had never paid a shilling, and upon writing to the town where she came from she found that her father was her only relative in the world. Mrs. J. looked upon her, therefore, as lawful prey.

This girl was a thorough Irish beauty, with dark blue eyes and black hair, a rather dingy skin, a pretty enough face, and having a well-formed figure, though rather thin; however, there was something taking about her, although she looked grave and sad. She was turned twelve years old.

The next I shall describe was Miss Jennings, a merry laughing blonde, very plump and pretty, with a profusion of light hair. She had been brought up by her grandmother, who paid very little. This girl was about eleven and ripe for a frolic.

The last of the trio, Miss Bellew, was a tall, handsome girl of fifteen, nicely made, but a little too slight if anything. She was dark and swarthy, a brunette, in fact; but there was soul in her black eyes, and withal a look of languor quite enchanting. As for the little cousins, they were mere chubby children.

Such being our party, and chocolate and fruit with plenty of cakes and bonbons being served on the lawn by Phoebe and Chloe, we all soon became great friends. The refection concluded, and leaving Cecilia to entertain Mrs. J., I took the bevy of young girls to see the poultry yard and then the ponies. I had previously given Phoebe a hint to let the stallion into the mare's compartment, so that when we arrived the animals were in the very act—a sight which provoked the astonishment and laughter of the little girls and made Miss Marshall look very pale and grave while Misses Jennings and Bellew blushed up to the eyes.

"Oh, come away, come away," cried Miss Marshall, turning sharp round; but I stopped her.

"Why should they go away, my dear?" I asked.

"Because, because—" and then stopped.

"Because what?" said I.

"Because—I think you are a naughty bad man, Sir Charles," sobbed the foolish girl, and burst into tears.

"Oh Bella," cried all the other girls in a breath, "for shame, to speak so to Sir Charles. Never mind her, sir, she is always like that, a miserable thing to spoil fun."

"I am sorry to hear it," said I. "When I invite young ladies here I expect them to be cheerful and polite, and if they are not we have a birch rod quite handy."

Mrs. J. coming up at this moment, the girls all ran to tell her how Bella had behaved.

"In that case, Sir Charles," said the good lady, "we must commence the sports by giving her a good flogging."

Miss Marshall turned paler than she was before at this announcement.

Mrs. J. had a heavy hand, as she knew by dear bought experience, but she was of a dogged and sulky disposition and said nothing.

"How now, miss," cried Mrs. J., "say you are very sorry immediately or you shall be flogged at once."

No answer.

"Will you apologise or not?"

No answer.

"Yes, yes; I see we must make you speak then. Here, my good girl," said she, addressing Phoebe. "You are strong, take her up, and you, my little lasses, come, hold her legs."

And the refractory Bella being mounted, and her clothes thrown over her head, Mrs. J. selected from a new birch broom a goodly handful of twigs, and tying them with a ribband prepared for action.

We all now had a full view of her well-formed white buttocks and thighs; and the other girls, who seemed to enjoy the scene, held her legs so wide apart that we could see her pouting cunny and all the regions thereabout.

Bella, meanwhile, bounding and struggling to be free, only exposed her charms the more.

"Now," said Mrs. J., "you young hussy, for whom I have never yet received a shilling, I'll teach you manners, you wretched pauper, I will."

And she commenced flogging her till the stubborn girl roared for mercy and her white bottom glowed again.

"No—no—no," cried Mrs. J., giving a tremendous cut each time she said the word, "I will flog this devil out of you before I have done."

"Oh, dear madam, pray forgive me. Oh—oh—oh—oh; kind Sir Charles, do intercede! Oh, I shall die; oh! oh!"

But by this time I had got too much interested to interfere and quieted Cecilia with a gesture, and the operation proceeded.

Large weals rose up on her flesh, the blood started and ran down her thighs, and at length, with a prolonged shriek, she fainted.

"There," cried Mrs J., drawing a long breath, "take her away, and don't let me see the slut till it is time to leave."

But at the sight of the poor fainting girl I relented, and lifting her up bore her to a couch in my room; and having unfastened her dress and bathed her temples with Hungary water, I left her and returned to my company. Preparations were just being made for a game at hunt-the-slipper, and every one being seated on the lawn I ran round the circle, every now and then feeling for the slipper under the legs of the girls.

The little screams, the shouts of laughter, and the fun was tremendous; for you may be sure that every girl in her turn felt my hand between her naked thighs.

With some it was a hasty grasp, but with others I lingered and fairly frigged, pretending all the while that I was sure they had the slipper. To see the little Agnes and Augusta laugh at being so tickled was delightful; and the conscious blushes of the misses Jennings and Bellew were equally enchanting. As for Miss Bellew, her languishing black eyes shot forth scintillations of light as she fairly spent in my hand; but the little Jennings was less precocious and merely laughed at the fun.

Altogether it was a most fucktious romp, and made me so amorous that I at length proposed a game of hide-and-seek for a change, and unperceived beckoned to Cecilia; we both ran to hide.

Having retired into a deep cluster of trees and shrubs, I put my little wife on her knees and was into her in a moment, at the same time calling out "whoop." Into the wood they all came shouting and laughing, but could not for a long time find us; at length Agnes and Augusta taking an opposite vista to their companions, came suddenly upon us just as my climax came. I immediately drew out, and thus gave them a complete view of that red headed staff, at the sight of which, and of their cousin's ivory posteriors shining in the sun, they stopped, turned round, and bounded off to their companions, crying out:

"Oh! Miss Jennings, oh Miss Bellew, here's Sir Charles doing to cousin Cecilia just what the horse did to the mare!"

Then we heard a whispering; and presently I became aware, by the rustling of the branches, that the girls were placing themselves in ambush to see all they could.

The idea of such beauteous spectators brought me up to the mark again in a moment, and at it we went in good style. Every now and then a little eager face would peep out from among the leaves and then be withdrawn in great trepidation, which caused such a thrill to run through my veins that I brought that second embrace to a conclusion much sooner than I had a mind to.

No sooner did they see that I was beginning to button up again but they scampered off in different directions, pretending to be looking for us. Meanwhile, we shifted our quarters and again cried out "whoop."

This time they ran up to catch us, pretending, the little sly pussies, that they had had such a hunt for us. Being now Miss Bellew's turn to hide, we all remained on the lawn while she ran into the wood. It now occurred to me for the first time that Mrs. J. and Phoebe had disappeared, nor could I anywhere see Chloe.

So that when Miss Bellew's "whoop" summoned us to the wood, instead of looking for her I hunted in every direction for the truants, and at length, at some distance from the spot where the game was going on, I fancied I saw a bit of blue silk between the trees; and bending my steps to a thick clump of hazel I approached softly, and lo! on a little patch of mossy turf, in a hollow space, I espied the excellent lady doing a little bit of tribadism with Phoebe. They were at the height of enjoyment; Phoebe uppermost.

"Ah, ah, my sweet girl," Mrs. J. was sighing out. "That is it. Ah, ah, now you've found the right place, at the—top. Oh, bliss; ah-oh. Ur-r-r! oh, how nice; continue to roll your tongue round and round."

Then slapping the beautiful great white bottom of Phoebe, which was presented to her, she continued, "Oh, what heavenly charms, what a skin! what glorious white globes! what a delicious little nether mouth, let me kiss your sweet cunny; let me thrust my tongue in and taste your spendings. Ah, this is bliss indeed. Ur-r-r-r!"

Then Phoebe began.

"Ah, dear madam, what are you doing? oh lud, it do make me feel so funny loike. Oh, my, ain't it nice though? Oh—"

A gush of spending from Mrs. J. stopped her mouth, while the movements became furious. Phoebe rolled off on to the grass and the two women lay without sense or motion beyond the heaving of their breasts. I was much amused and retreated without being discovered.

I now thought of Chloe, and wanting my snuffbox which I had left indoors, I went for it, when the first thing that met my eyes was the little girl trying to console the naughty Miss Marshall, who was lying on her side on a couch, with her face to the wall, while the good-natured Chloe was bathing the poor flayed bum of the young lady.

I approached softly, and with my finger on my lip motioned to Chloe to take no notice, and seated myself about a yard from them.

As Miss Marshall's clothes were turned up above her waist, I was able to contemplate at my ease the symmetrical proportions of her sylph-like form.

The fine contour of her virgin rose and the little rose bud attached thereto all was before me.

Presently she spoke. "How kind you are to me, dearest Chloe," she said, languidly. "I begin to feel in less pain now, but what is very singular, I, who never had any sensations in that part before, now feel a most singular itching between the legs—in the slit, you know."

"Just here?" cried Chloe, laughing and putting her finger in.

"Oh, yes, yes. Ah, how nice it feels now you touch it. Oh, I feel so ashamed," and she covered her face with her hand.

Chloe withdrew her hand.

"I did not mean to offend you," she said.

"Offend me; oh, no. Let me feel that dear little finger again."

I approached on my hands and knees and quickly substituted my finger for Chloe's.

"Oh, my dear girl," she cried, "oh, how very nice, but I feel quite ashamed."

Then, as I touched her clitoris, a shiver ran through her frame. She threw herself over on her back, expanded her thighs, and, with her eyes still closed, murmured, "Come, come here, darling girl, on my bosom, on my bosom."

I placed Chloe there in a moment, and then tossing up the little girl's clothes, I began toying with her lovely buttocks. Then, kneeling up behind her, I directed my fiery steed strait at Miss Marshall's maidenhead.

The first push took me in about an inch, but, with a

shriek and a start, the Irish girl opened her eyes, commencing with, "Oh, my dear Chloe, how you hurt me, I—"

Then seeing me she struggled to get up and turned pale with terror.

"Oh, for heaven's sake, let me get up—oh, goodness! Mercy! mercy!"

These ejaculations followed every thrust, for I would not let go but made Chloe lie with all her weight on the little Marshall until I was at length fairly into her body. Then, indeed, I rolled Chloe on one side and extending myself on the bosom of the girl and grasping her tightly in my arms I consummated the defloration.

At first terrified, then angry, she finished by hugging her ravisher in her arms and covering him with kisses.

All this, which has taken so long to tell, happened in an incredibly short space of time, so that I was hardly missed ere I reappeared among my young friends.

Mrs. J. and Phoebe now joined us, looking very innocent, and I having interceded for Miss Marshall, she and Chloe were sent for and joined in the sports. I had quite tamed the angry petulant girl and she occasionally glanced at me with a look full of meaning and of indefinable tenderness. Her passions were aroused and she had tasted of the tree of knowledge.

It being now eight o'clock, supper was served up to us with a profusion of all the delicacies of the season and the choicest wines and liqueurs. After this we had a dance and a game at blindman's buff, and then my guests took their departure, Mrs. J. declaring that she had never enjoyed herself more! (Glancing at Phoebe.)

"Well then," said I, "suppose you all come again next Thursday?"

"Oh, I shall be enchanted, I am sure, to do so, Sir Charles," said Mrs. J., "but I suppose you will not want to see Miss Marshall any more?"

"On the contrary," I remarked, "she has quite made the *amende honorable,* and we are now very good friends. Is it not so, young lady?" I added, turning to her.

A burning blush suffused her pale face, but she managed to stammer out, "Oh, yes, Madame, I am sure Sir Charles is most kind. I am very sorry I behaved as I did, but if you will let me come next time I promise never so to offend again, even if there are fifty horses and mares instead of one."

With that I kissed them all round, and handing them into my coach bid them good night.

Adieu, dear friend.

To Lais

Lady Cecilia has fallen in love, and with a very Daphnis too, the beautiful little brother of the charming Phoebe. He came here the other day to see his sister, and prodigiously took the fancy of my lady. As we are far too philosophical, in this our terrestrial paradise, to agitate ourselves with such absurd passions as jealousy, I left Cecilia to do as she liked; so she has engaged the pretty fellow, who is just fourteen and the image of his sister, as her body page, but instead of putting him in livery, has dressed him à la Watteau, a style of costume at once simple and elegant.

Of course, she made his sister give him a good scrubbing and combing before he mounted his new clothes, and now powdered, perfumed, and dressed he looks fit for a princess. Phoebe is hugely pleased that Jack is to stay here, and as for little Chloe, she evidently has some very sinister designs on his virtue.

I told Cecilia that I congratulated her on such an acquisition and hoped she would not object to my seeing some of the performances. She laughed, and replied, "Oh, see all you like, my dear Charles, only don't let the boy know at first, as he is very bashful and timid."

I promised compliance.

A few days afterwards, as I lay on the banks of the lake listlessly feeding the carp, Phoebe came running to me, and having seated herself quite out of breath by my side, she told me that Cecilia and her brother were amusing themselves in the grotto, in the grove of beeches, and if I would make haste I might see something that would amuse me. So, throwing my arm round Phoebe's waist, I accompanied her, going round to the opposite side to the entrance. We looked through a chink in the rockwork and could both see and hear all that passed.

First I observed Cecilia seated on the mossy bank, and holding the boy, whose breeches were down, between her naked thighs, his hands were toying with her bubbies.

While she, having tucked up his fine cambric shirt, with her right hand caressed his little stiff thing and with her left patted his pretty dimpled soft and girlish bottom.

"Oh, you dear little fellow," said she, "what a beautiful figure you have got, your waist is so small, your bottom so plump, dimpled, and rounded, and your skin so soft; you have such a lovely face, your hair is so silky luxuriant, and beautiful, and you have such little hands and feet, surely nature quite intended you for a girl, only she gave you this little saucy cock instead of something else, which, however, I am very glad of, as you will be able to play with me. Dear boy, do you like me to tickle it?"

"Oh, yes, my lady," cried the lad, "very much indeed, and I do love these little breasts so, do let me kiss them."

And pulling her bubbies out he buried his face between them.

"But," she exclaimed, "you have not looked at this other little secret place—but perhaps, you have seen girls before?"

"Why, my lady, to say the truth, I have, but only little ones. I should like to see your ladyship's beautiful cunt very much."

"Oh, fie, naughty boy, do not use such naughty words. But look, here it is."

And she straddled open her legs.

"Feel it with your pretty little hand. Oh, you dear fellow, that is nice; now lie down upon me and I will show you what love is."

And grasping his beautiful buttocks, she drew him to her and he slipped in with ease.

"Now, dear boy, move up and down, that's it, my little stallion; you are, I see, an apt pupil."

Then holding open those white hemispheres, she inserted her delicate finger into his little rosy orifice behind, and entwining her lovely limbs round his loins, they were presently bounding and heaving with delight.

The sight was so exhilirating to both Phoebe and myself that I lifted up her clothes, and still contemplating the ardent young lovers, commenced the same game myself.

Now, whatever the ancients may have thought on the subject, I must confess I have never seen what the peculiar point of attraction could be in having beautiful boys, as they unquestionably did; yet when I saw that lovely young bottom bounding up and down, and Cecilia's wanton finger frigging away, a strange dizziness seized me and I felt a lust, stronger than the lust for women, lay hold of me.

But one cannot be perfectly happy in this world long together, so that it happened that just at the height of titillation, my climax came and I sent a gushing stream into her bowels.

Cecilia and her Daphnis having also died away in bliss, we beat a retreat, to prevent discovery.

Thus you see, my dear Lais, that like a true Epicurean, I never let slip any pleasure within my reach.

I think it behoves us to live while we may and give full scope to those delicious sensual appetites which we can only enjoy for so short a time.

Hoping soon to have the happiness of seeing you here,

I remain,
Your devoted Admirer.

To Thalia

I believe, my dear girl, I gave you a full relation of all that had passed here during this last three months on the occasion of that delicious clandestine visit you paid me about a week ago. I am now going to continue the narrative, which I hope will prove edifying to my dear little girl.

You must know then, my love, that I was most anxious to become better acquainted with my wife's young cousins, and as she was quite willing I should do just as I liked with them, I sent a letter to Mrs. J. requesting that they might pass a few days with us. They arrived accordingly the next morning.

"Now, Cecilia," said I, "I want you to leave us entirely to ourselves; so do you go and make a few calls in the neighbourhood."

To this the dear little wife at once consented, so taking each of my little cousins by the hand, I proposed we should go a nutting (you know what a famous nut wood I have here). The little creatures were delighted and skipped merrily along. Arrived at the wood, they began climbing the trees in search of the nuts, showing me their little fat bottoms and legs without the least concern.

As soon as they had gathered a pretty considerable basketful, I proposed that we should seat ourselves under a spreading tree and eat them.

"Now, my little loves," said I, "while you are cracking your nuts, I will try and amuse you."

The pretty creatures in seating themselves drew up their legs so as to make a lap to hold their nuts, and as Mrs. J. had taken care their petticoats should be short, I had a full view of all their youthful charms. Plump, white little thighs, between which pouted their rosy slits, a luscious sight, enough to fire the veins of an anchorite.

But, as I have no pretensions to that holy character, I was beside myself with desire and ready to eat them up altogether. However, I restrained my impatience with much ado and began to beat about the bush.

"Now I daresay, my darlings, you would like to know where the babies come from?"

"Oh!" cried the little Agnes," I know very well."

Then whispering mysteriously in my ear, "They come out of the parsley bed."

"Nonsense," cried Augusta, who had overheard her, "no such thing, I know better than that; they come from the mother, do they not, Sir Charles?"

"Yes, my dear," said I sententiously, "indeed they do; but can you tell me how they got into the mother's stomach in the first place, and how they get out in the second?"

"Why, no, Sir Charles, I cannot tell what made them get there, nor do I exactly know how they come into the world; some of the girls at our school say that the mother's stomach opens and lets them out, but I really do not quite know."

"Would you like me to tell you, then?"

"Oh, dear sir, of all things, do, do, tell us all about it."

"Well, then," said I laughing, "I must begin at the beginning."

"Yes, yes, that's it," cried the little girls in a breath, cracking their nuts and very wickedly throwing the shells at an unoffending sparrow who was hopping about near them.

"Very well," said I. "In the beginning the heaven and the earth were created—"

"Oh, lud, we know all about that, you see. But what has that got to do with it?" cried the saucy Augusta.

"In the beginning the heaven and the earth were created," I went on, dogmatically, "every creeping thing and all that therein is, male and female. Now, can you tell me why they were made male and female?"

My young pupils looked puzzled.

"I will tell you," said I gravely, "they were made male and female that they may be joined together, just as you saw the pony stallion and the mare joined, and thus propagate their kind. There is nothing wrong or indelicate in their doing this; are we not told to 'be fruitful and multiply'?"

"Of course we are," cried the girls in a breath.

"Well, then," I continued, "Miss Marshall was wrong in wishing you to come away the other day, for, my dear children, you were contemplating one of the works of nature. Now you know, I daresay, that little boys are not made like little girls?"

"Oh, yes; we know that."

"Well, shall I tell you why they are not?"

"Oh, yes; do, do."

"Well then, because that little innocent thing of the boy's is capable, in the man, of becoming a great thing, and nature has ordained that he shall feel a particular pleasure in putting that part of him into that little female opening, of which I see two specimens before me."

They both blushed and pulled down their clothes.

"When it is in, he moves up and down, and in doing so gives great pleasure to the female, and after a time he discharges into her a thick milky, or rather gruel-like, fluid, which is the seed; this being received into the womb and fecundating the ovaries or eggs, which are in her fallopian tubes—so called from a learned doctor named Fallopius, who discovered them—the egg descends into the womb and begins to grow, and nine months after a child is born."

"Oh, but that is very funny, and very wonderful," they cried.

"My dear girls, it is not funny, but it is wonderful."

They both looked very thoughtful; at length Augusta said, "And would there be any harm in your showing us what this wonderful thing which makes the babies is like?"

"On the contrary, my dear little girl, here it is!" and unbuttoning my breeches, out sprung my truncheon as stiff as a carrot.

"Oh, gracious, what a funny thing," was the ejaculation which escaped them as they approached and began to handle Mr. Pasquin.

"That is the true maker of babies, my darlings, is he not a fine dolly? Play with him a little and soon you will see what the seed is like, and remember every drop may contain a baby."

"Oh, the funny, big, red-headed thing," exclaimed the little girls, rubbing and pulling it about. "And what are these two balls for, Sir Charles?"

The New Epicurean • 67

"They, my dears, contain the seed, which is formed in the loins at first, and then descending through those balls pass into the woman."

"Then," said Augusta, "when people are said to be in love, it means that they want to join those parts together."

"Just so, that is the end of all marriages."

"But," argued little Agnes. "do ladies really like to have it done to them?"

"Of course they do, my dear, if they love the man they marry."

"But why do they like it?"

"Because they feel a strange pleasure in the act."

"Really, how very odd," both exclaimed.

"Not at all," said I, "let me just tickle you a little in that part and you will soon know what I mean."

"Indeed," said Augusta, "I know already, for when you did that to me while playing hunt-the-slipper, I thought it very nice."

At this admission, as they had not ceased caressing that great erect prick, a *jet d'eau* spouted forth, covering both their hands with the warm fluid, at which they both gave a little scream of astonishment and then fell examining it attentively.

"And every drop of this curious stuff contains a baby?" enquired Augusta.

"Every drop," said I.

"Who would have thought it," she continued, much interested, "how very, very curious."

"Having now told you all about that part of the business, my dear children," said I, "I must now go on to tell you that the pleasures of love are manifold, and I will explain to you what some of those pleasures are.

"First of all, is the pleasure derived from titillation

with the finger, as practised by school-girls. But this, though very exquisite when first commenced, palls after a year or two, deadens the sensation of the little cunny and, what is worse, injures the health. The blooming cheeks will then become pale, the bright eyes sunken, the skin yellow and flabby. Therefore that is not the enjoyment I intend to recommend to you, my dears.

"Secondly, there is tribadism, or the love of one girl for another, which leads them mutually to gratify each other's desires by kissing and licking that salacious part of their bodies. No doubt the bliss is great, but I never yet met a girl who would assert that a tribade could satisfy her. It is very exciting, no doubt, but after working the nervous sensibility up to the highest tension, it leaves you still tingling with desire—longing, wishing for something you know not what, but forever unsatisfied. Like that unhappy Tantalus, forever plunged to the chin in water but unable to drink; so I cannot recommend tribadism.

"Thirdly, there is the true and right kind of bliss, when two young creatures of opposite sexes meet, kiss, caress, and coo; and time, place, and opportunity occurring, join together those luscious parts of their persons. Add to this the pursuit of pleasure *en règle,* and to these delights of love I will introduce you."

The little girls, who had paid great attention, came nestling up to me, saying, "Oh, what a dear, nice man you are, Sir Charles; I do love you so very much, you are so kind."

I kissed them both, and with my two hands patting each of their little peach-like nether beauties, while they played with dolly of the red head, I continued, "But before I introduce you to your young lover that is to be, I want to say a few words on incentives. Now, while I disapprove of fingering, tribadism, gamahuching, and the like when intended as a sole means of satisfying natural lust, I think such acts may be practised if the natural completion in a hearty fuck is to follow.

"None of these acts will then do you the least harm, because the effect of fucking is to tranquillize the nerves and produce a delicious calmness and serenity. Having now, therefore, concluded my sermon, I will go without delay and find Master Jack, who I am very sure is up to some mischief, either stealing my peaches or fighting amain the cocks in the poultry yard, setting the dogs at old Mother Jukes' cat, or teasing Chloe. However, I will bring him captive to your feet."

I found our young Daphnis at the cottage. But let me describe him to you, for you did not see him when here.

You are to imagine then, a beautiful young girl, but with male, instead of female, attributes, with a polished skin like alabaster, and whose exquisite face is a perfect oval; imagine a girl of fourteen with large melting eyes, black lashes, pencilled eyebrows, *nez retroussé,* small coral-lipped mouth, teeth like pearls, and dimpled cheeks tinted with the softest blush of the rose.

Imagine a profusion of light brown curling hair, powdered and tied by a cherry-coloured ribbon, rather narrow chest, small waist, and voluptuous hips and accessories; in fine a charming picture full of grace and elegance, dressed à la Watteau.

I found the young rascal lying at the foot of a cherry tree, up which Chloe had clambered, lazily eating the fruit she threw down to him, while ever and anon he languidly raised his eyes to look at that other fruit which her short dress rendered so conspicuous.

As I conducted him into the nut wood, the two sweet

children ran to meet us, and then looked shy, shook their shoulders and blushed. Not so the boy; he went up to them with some gallant speech or other not now worth repeating, and soon they were at high romps on the grass, to my great delight. After a little more of this by-play, he began to take all sorts of liberties.

They retaliated, so that, in a quarter of an hour, the acquaintance was so far improved that they had got his breeches off, his shirt up above his waist; then Augusta falling over the root of a tree, up went her legs; he fell upon her, and then—then at it he went in good style, little Agnes behind him tickling his marbles and Augusta hugging and kissing him with all her strength.

The sight was most fucktious. His beautiful girlish bottom bounding up and down, its peach-like cheeks trembling from their very plumpness, his stiff little cock, now in, now out; her plump thighs shining white against the greensward and her lovely shaped, hairless cunny. Add to this the various beauties her sister also displayed, and I think you will admit that a lovelier picture could not well be conceived, and I would have given fifty guineas to have had Watteau here at that moment to paint the scene.

At this enchanting moment, seeing Phoebe crossing a neighbouring copse, I called her, and putting her on all fours she soon became a performer in this *fête champètre*. She bounded and wriggled, I thrust; the children shouted and laughed. Sure there never was such a merry luscious scene. But as all things, even the most delightful, must have an end, and Phoebe had been very skillfully manipulating me for some minutes, amidst ah's and oh's and Oh my dear love's, and sighs and coos of delirious bliss, she died away in extasy. Nor were the young ones long after us. As for Augusta, she fairly ground her teeth in joy.

To Helen

What an age it seems, beloved Helen, since I last saw your sylph-like form enlivening these shades. The very trees seem to droop in your absence. Cannot you come and pass a few days with us? When I think of the austere, cold-hearted man they have married you to, I feel oppressed with a sadness which no delights can dispel. Come then, my lovely Helen, and rejoice me with a view of your charms once more.

You ask me for news of our doings here; and though I have always some new adventure to relate, I should do so with more pleasure could I but identify you with this paradise.

Cecilia and I diversify our amusements. To this end she has the most cavalier servant in the world, and I two sweet girls who are entirely at my disposal.

I wish you could see Phoebe and Chloe, for you would scarcely find anywhere more lovely creatures.

Then there are my wife's little cousins, Augusta and Agnes, who come from school sometimes, and who I have initiated in all the mysteries of Venus.

Yesterday we had a garden party, consisting of Mrs. J. and three of her pupils, Mesdames Bellew, Marshall, and Jennings, besides the cousins.

The sports consisted of swinging, blind-man's-buff, hunt-the-slipper, hide-and-seek, and concluded with a bath in the lake and supper on the lawn.

My new swing was hailed with acclamations by the young ladies, who with Chloe and Phoebe, not forgetting Lady Cecilia, were speedily seated therein. This filled up every seat, which relieved Mrs. J., poor woman, as she had no desire, she said, to make an exhibition of herself at her age. And *entre nous,* she is a little *passé,* and has, besides, such a tremendous black bearskin in a certain quarter that the sight of so grim an affair would have spoiled the view. As for our little Daphnis (that is his *nom d'amour,* you know, otherwise he rejoices in the vulgar epithet of "Jack"), he was in raptures and ran along the line of beauty trying to see all he could. Then, oh, the laughter, the little screams, the coquettish attempts to prevent him seeing their charms, and the badinage and saucy jokes that were bandied about, made up a scene which quite beggars description. Then as soon as the swing began to move and swung high in the air, the fun grew fast and furious and the sight was not only exciting but also most singular; for as I sat underneath, as they swung over my head, I could not see anything but bottoms, thighs, legs, and pretty little feet, all of a row. Occasionally, to obtain a firmer seat, one of them would give a wriggle or twist, which showed me some new charm—a nymphoe or clitoris would pop out—and with each movement I discovered new beauties. When they were tired of this fun, we played blind-man's-buff, I of course being blind man. The little pussies were pretty rough in their play, pushing me about at their pleasure and taking all manner of liberties; but no sooner had I caught one of them but I took my revenge, putting my hand up her clothes without ceremony. Feeling a luscious pouting, little cunny, on which a soft down was beginning to sprout, I at once recognized it and cried out, "Ah! I know you, it is Miss Bellew."

"Right, right!" shouted the merry voices, and pulling off the handkerchief I at once made her pay toll before them all. You will observe we went far beyond kissing here. In fact, tossing up the young lady's petticoats, I pushed her gently on her hands and knees, and having long been primed was into her in a moment. As for the others, with many a gay repartee, they seated themselves in a circle and watched the performance.

Poor Miss Bellew, as you may suppose (though nothing loth to the thing itself), would have preferred a more private place. But seeing there was no escape, she submitted with a good grace. Indeed, she need not have distressed herself, for her companions, stimulated by what they saw, were soon so fully occupied themselves as to pay little attention to us. Cecilia led Daphnis into a little grove, sacred to Priapus; Phoebe and Mrs. J. disappeared down an avenue; Augusta and Chloe became little tribades for the time; while the others were all frigging away right and left.

Sure the isle of Capri in the days of Tiberius could have shown no more voluptuous scenes than those which startled the very birds in the trees from their propriety.

But, alas! this is but a terrestrial Elysium, and we soon found that we were neither gods nor goddesses. Half an hour satisfied all our desires for that bout, and all were soon seated for a game of hunt-the-slipper, which passed off with the usual pleasantries of frigging and feeling, in which I allowed Daphnis to share, and the young wag set us all in a roar by insisting that as he could not find the slipper he was sure Mrs. J. had put it up her cunt, and in spite of all her protestations he would feel for himself, which I have no doubt that cunning and salacious dame relished most heartily.

You must know, my love, that Mrs. J. is still a fine woman, who, ten or twelve years ago, has often had me panting on her bosom. Phew! those days are gone by; I require more juvenile stuff to give me a stiffener now. Then came the romping game of hide-and-seek, which produced great fun. But by far the most *recherché* scene of all was the bath.

You know that lovely lake, my Helen; for 'twas in its crystal water we first enjoyed love's blisses together.

In a few minutes we were all undressed and sportively splashing each other, swimming, kissing, tickling, fucking. Oh, ye gods, what a scene it was. Such perfect abandon I do verily believe was never witnessed, even at the Dionysian festivals of ancient Greece. But one thing was wanting to make us mad as the satyrs and bacchantes of those times. And that one thing I resolved to have—wine. I despatched Phoebe and Daphnis for a dozen of Burgundy. The cup circulated; we all became intoxicated; we performed prodigies of lust, gamahuched, and did everything that the most wanton imagination can conceive; so that coming at length out of the lake, in which some of the girls were near being drowned, none of the party save Cecilia, Mrs. J., and myself could dress ourselves. Calling in the aid then of old Mrs. Jukes, we first put Phoebe, Chloe, and Daphnis to bed. Then, huddling on the clothes of the other young ladies, we got them, as best we might, to the coach and sent them home at seven o'clock that summer's evening, as completely drunk as ever was a lady of pleasure in Covent Garden.

As for Cecilia and myself, we partook of a light supper, went to bed, and were soon in the arms of Morpheus.

To Livia

I find from my excellent friend, Mrs. J., that she has given you an elaborate account of our late doings here, when we emulated the ancients with our Bacchanalian orgies. The finish of that scene was not, I must confess, at all to my taste, and we all suffered more or less the next day for our excess. I have therefore determined not to proceed to such lengths again.

Yesterday, being the breaking up for the holidays at Mrs. J.'s, I proposed to her to invite the whole school of twenty-six young ladies. But not to injure the interests of the good lady, I promised that any little amorous fun that took place should be covert and accidental, apparently.

That if any of the innocent ones saw aught that might shock their notions of propriety, it should be so managed that they would never think it was a premeditated affront.

To this end I caused the statues of Priapus to be wreathed with laurel and ivy about the middle. I locked up all the naughty books and pictures, and as it was not intended to proceed to any voluptuous extremities while the young ladies were with us, I introduced on this occasion an excellent band of musicians, who were located in a tent pitched on a spot where they could observe little of the proceedings. From Ranelagh Gardens I brought Jackson, the fireworks man, at an expense of twenty pounds. During the morning he was very busy hanging variegated lamps on both sides of every verdant valley, and the taste he displayed was wonderful. The weather continued delicious, clear and warm, so it promised to be very effective. Meantime a sumptuous refection was prepared. The new and old swing were dusted and got ready, the fountains were set a playing, and when at three o'clock the young ladies arrived all was in readiness. Lady Cecilia looked charming in a white satin commode and quilted hoop of pink silk; her hair was delicately powdered, and Renaud, that prince of coiffeurs, had coquettishly placed a real rose on one side of her head, which had a vastly pretty effect. As for me I wore my grey tiffling coat, a pompadour waistcoat, grey satin breeches and silks, with my best pair of diamond buckles in my shoes. I also, in honour of my company, mounted my gold-hilted sword, mechlin lace ruffles, bag and solitaire.

Upon the arrival of the school we first of all discussed the viands set out on the grass under the shade of a widespreading elm. Six and twenty girls sitting on the lawn, you will readily suppose, could not all place themselves so correctly but what I got many a sly peep at legs, thighs, and cunnies I had never seen before; and the best of it was they were not the least aware of it, nor did the knowing ones—Mesdames Marshall, Jennings, Bellew, Augusta and Agnes—venture to give them a hint; so there I sat, eating the wing of a chicken and viewing the secret charms of four or five of the finest girls in the world.

The repast over, we proceeded to walk round the grounds, and when we came to the terminal figure of Priapus, the god of the garden, they all came to a halt; and while they considered him attentively, they asked me to explain all about his worship in ancient times, which I did to their entire satisfaction.

One tall, elegant girl of fourteen, Miss Medley, showed

more curiosity than the others, and lingered behind to have a private view of the divinity. I had no doubt she wanted to see what it was the ivy concealed; so after we had got a little further I pretended that I had left my snuff box indoors, and deputing Cecilia to show them everything I stealthily returned and creeping up among the foliage at the back of the statue beheld the ivy removed and Miss Medley, on tiptoe, trying to rub her cunny against the marble Priape. Altering my position, therefore, so that she could see from my waist to my knees, but not my face, which the leaves concealed, I pulled out my own priape, which I handled till it was as big as the rural god's. She was some time before she saw it, but at length, when she did (supposing it was one of the musicians who was standing behind a tree for a necessary purpose), she recovered the statue, and placing herself behind it peeped out to see all that she could without being seen. Of course I shook the staff about and showed it off to the best advantage. She (not knowing I had seen her) displayed no alarm, nothing but intense curiosity; but I saw her right hand disappear under her clothes in a very mysterious manner; and from that moment I knew she was mine. With two strides I was beside her, finger on lip. She looked petrified with terror and shame, but I soon reassured her.

"My dear girl," said I, "this is what you want" (placing it in her hand), "not the marble one, which is only to look at. Let me show you what use it is put to, and I promise not to tell Mrs. J. anything I have seen."

"Oh, pray, good sir, what would you do? Consider my honour, my virtue. Ah, my goodness, what will become of me?"

"Why, certainly," said I, "it would not be very pleasant for your mamma to be told how you have acted, and to look so long at a naked man when by quickly walking away, you would scarcely have seen him. Oh, fie, miss."

"Oh, but, Sir Charles, you will not tell, will you?"

"Certainly not, if you comply with my wishes."

And I clasped her firm posteriors with one hand and her beautiful glowing cunny with the other.

"But, Sir Charles, will it not hurt very much?"

"Well, it will hurt a little at first, but the pleasure will soon drown the pain."

She was silent, but I felt her hand tremble as she squeezed my great prick between her taper white fingers.

That was enough, so lifting her in my arms I bore her to a little grove in which was a tool house never visited by anybody but the gardeners, and here putting a bundle of matting on a turned over wheelbarrow, I deposited the fair girl and was soon driving away at her maidenhead.

She bit her lip with the pain but did not cry out, which I considered a good omen; so caressingly slapping her thighs and handling her breasts and buttocks, I soon found a sensible moisture in that luscious part into which I was forcing my way—the darling girl was spending. Soon she gave tongue in delirious ejaculation: "Ah! where am I? Oh! how nice it is. Ah—oh—bl—bliss! Ah, oh, ur—r—r—r!"

And grinding her teeth, she nearly squeezed the breath out of me, hugging me with her arms and entwining her thighs around my loins with a tiger-like strength that nearly broke my back.

This girl, who had large open blue eyes and a confident bold air, had evidently found what she had long required, only she did not know it, and that was a good stiff cock. And having found it, she had a good mind to keep it, for my crisis having come and desiring to withdraw, she would by no means let me, but planted her touches so wantonly and with such good effect that positively (a rare thing at my time of life) I got a second erection within ten minutes of the departure of the first.

She now grew quite bold and whispered me not to let it come so soon.

It consequently happened that we lingered half an hour in that delightful spot.

As soon as the beauteous Miss Medley had a little recovered herself, I raised her up and offering my arm went in search of her companions.

"Well?" said I, "you find the real surpasses the *beau ideal?*"

"Not the same thing at all," she whispered, pressing my arm.

"What pains me is the reflection that just as I have won, I am to lose you. You go home tomorrow, do you not?"

"Yes, that is so," she said; then hesitating a little, she added, "but if you really desire it, that need not prevent your seeing me, as I live no further off than Richmond, and there are numerous lovely secluded spots where we could meet."

I stopped involuntarily with surprise, then catching her up in my arms I covered her with kisses, exclaiming, "Why, my angel, this is more than my fondest hopes could have suggested. Do you really mean what you say? Or, come now, acknowledge that you are laughing at me."

"I, not the least in the world."

"Then you really mean what you say."

"*Ma foi,* yes; I find you a gallant man."

I took off my hat and made a lower bow to Miss Medley than I ever made to a little miss before.

Then renewing our conversation, she gave me full directions when I was to meet her, on what days, and at what hour. By the time she had finished we found ourselves in the midst of the merrymakers.

"Why, goodness gracious," cried a dozen voices at once, "where have you two been all this while? We had quite lost you both."

Poor Miss Medley blushed, but I came to the rescue, quickly saying, "You know, I went indoors for my snuff box; in returning I made a detour through the maze to see if the lamps had been hung to my mind and found Miss Medley, who had quite lost herself in its intricate winding and shouted to me to show her the way out, which after some time I was able to do, and here we are."

This explanation satisfied the majority, but I saw Misses Marshall and Jennings exchange a meaning look, which I had no difficulty in reading, but of course took no notice.

We had interrupted a capital game at hide-and-seek, which was now continued.

It being Miss Jenning's turn to hide, away she tripped into the wood, but as she passed me she managed to squeeze a little crumpled billet, written in pencil, into my hand. As soon therefore as we heard "whoop," away we ran in every direction, and finding myself alone I seized the opportunity of reading it.

It was of a brevity perfectly Spartan: "The tool house."

To the tool house I therefore proceeded as fast as possible, taking care none of the huntresses should see which way I took and pondering all the way on those two words.

Had it been Miss Marshall, all would have been clear

enough, but what did the little Jennings know about the tool house?

In the midst of my cogitations I saw it before me.

With a hasty glance to see that no one had followed me, I sprang over the threshold and shot the bolt behind me, and at that moment was clasped in the arms of the amorous girl.

"Oh, dear Sir Charles," she exclaimed, "this is kind of you, but you did awaken my passions, you know, and having aroused them, you will love me a little, will you not?"

"My darling girl," I cried, kneeling at her feet and sliding my hands under her clothes, grasping her naked thighs, "can you doubt it?"

"Well, yes, dear Sir Charles, I did doubt, for you are such a roué and such a votary to promiscuous love that I feared you might overlook poor little me, and now that bold Miss Medley with her great blue eyes has ensnared you, for you don't suppose your tale of the maze deceived me in the least—"

"Really," said I, laughing.

"Oh, you are a terrible rake, Sir Charles."

"You flatter me," I said, with a low bow.

"And then," cried the impetuous girl, as her dark eyes flashed, "I have to contend against the charms of Lady Cecilia, and Phoebe, and little Chloe, and—"

"Stop, stop," I exclaimed, "and *halte la!* In these precincts sacred to Venus and Priapus the green-eyed monster jealousy is never allowed to intrude; my love extends to beauty wherever it is to be found, and like the bee I fly from flower to flower and extract the sweets from each; be satisfied then, my precious girl, with your own share, and you will, believe me, have no cause to complain." And I imprinted a rapturous kiss on her damask cheek.

"But we are wasting precious moments in words, *ma petite*, let us proceed to deeds, if you please."

And suiting the action to the word, I made her kneel upon the gardener's matting, which still remained on the wheelbarrow as I had left it, and tossing up her clothes exposed her voluptuous white hemispheres.

"Oh, my; good gracious," cried the girl, "is that the way it is done? I thought you would lie on my bosom."

"There are various methods, my angel," said I, beginning to push at the mark, "and as we become better acquainted I hope to instruct you in the thirty-five positions."

"*Juste ciel!*" ejaculated the pretty creature, "are there so many, then?"

"Oh, yes," I rejoined, "and each more delightful than the other."

And grasping her round the hips, I began to thrust in good earnest. She buckled to admirably, and merely giving a little "oh!" of pain now and then, straddled and aided my entrance all she could, so that in about ten minutes I rode in at a canter, winning the race by a length.

Then, as she felt the swelling head of my stiffening weapon in the innermost depths of her cunny, this enamoured girl gave full vent to her delight. She jutted out her great white bottom, she passed her hand underneath and felt the balls of love; she manipulated me in a thousand ways; she bounded, wriggled, and twisted, sighed and cooed; her breath came short, and murmuring out, "Ah, sweet bliss! Ah, it is Heaven! Heaven!" she spent; and my extatic movement, by a lucky chance coming at the same time, I sank forward on those white globes in a delirium of joy.

How long we should have lain thus, Venus only knows; but the sound of approaching footsteps roused us from our voluptuous trance. Hastily arranging my dress, I slipped out of the door and hid myself amongst the underwood. I had scarcely concealed myself when a bevy of young girls appeared, shouting out at the top of their voices.

"Miss Jennings, Miss Jennings!"

"Where can she have hid herself?" cried one.

"I declare," said another, "I am quite hot and tired with looking for her."

"I should not wonder if she is in this tool house," cried another, "let us see."

And pushing open the door, they led her out, looking very confused and as red as a peony.

"Why, gracious goodness me, Miss Jennings, what could have induced you to choose such a place to hide?"

"Rather say," answered the lovely girl, recovering her presence of mind, "how foolish you all look at having been baffled so long."

"Well, well, we have found you at last; so come along and let us have a game at hunt-the-slipper; we shall only just have time for one game before the fireworks, for see it is getting quite dark." And the laughing girls led her off.

I was preparing to follow, not wishing to lose my share of a game I liked so well, when suddenly I felt a little hand in mine, and turning looked down on the smiling, rosy face of little Chloe.

"What! you here?" I cried, astonished. "How's this?"

"Oh, don't be angry, your honour," said she. "I followed you and saw all that passed in the tool house through a chink in the door; but I will not tell."

"Oh, you saucy little pussy," I cried, patting her rosy cheek, "and what do you want of me now?"

"Ah, Sir Charles, that you must guess, you know."

"Egad," said I, "that I can discern quite well, you funny little thing; but tell me, do you then like to have me, better than young Daphnis. He, so young, so beautiful, so near your own age, I so old compared to yourself. Is this possible?"

"Why, to tell you the truth, Sir Charles, I have a stronger liking for you than for him. He is too pretty by half, too like a girl; besides you taught me all I know of love; you first awakened those feelings; it was your hand first caressed that secret part which now always thrills when I approach you. Oh, Sir Charles, young as I am, I have all a woman's feelings."

"Then, my dear little love, you shall have all a woman's pleasure. Come," and I led her into the wood, and laying on my back made her get over me.

"I am rather tired, my love," said I, "so you must do all the work."

"That I will, and with pleasure, dear Sir Charles; but oh, dear me, you are not stiff, hardly at all; but I will soon remedy that. Let me gamahuche you; and if you like, do you gamahuche me and then we shall soon be ready."

So saying, she turned round, presenting her lovely little bottom and pressing her young cunny to my lips, my tongue slipped in at once, while she, taking my languid prick in her rosy mouth, so skillfully titillated it that in a very few minutes I was ready for action.

Again, therefore, reversing her attitude, she mounted me and a delightful fuck ensued.

The whole affair did not occupy a quarter of an hour,

and this little act in the drama being concluded, we joined the revels.

I will not weary you with a recapitulation of all the frolic of hunt-the-slipper; suffice it to say that without any apparent offence against propriety, I managed to accidentally, as it were, feel many a virgin cunny and many a plump thigh that night.

The fête concluded with a country dance amidst a general illumination and superb display of fireworks. Supper was then served and my guests departed about twelve, much delighted with their visit.

When they were gone and Cecilia and I had retired to bed, we compared notes of our various adventures.

She, it appeared, had not been idle, and attaching herself to Daphnis and Miss Bellew, they retreated to the grotto where fucking and gamahuching occupied them for an hour. She had also much diverted herself with the innocence of a pretty little girl, nine years old, Clara, to whom she had privately shown the ponies, and after exciting the young thing with the sight and by lascivious touches, had finally gamahuched her and been gamahuched to their mutual satisfaction.

She laughed heartily at the conquest I had made of Miss Medley's heart and asked if I intended to go to Richmond?

I fancied there was rather more eagerness than usual in her manner, and as I knew her not to be troubled with jealousy, I could not quite understand it. But dissembling my surprise, I answered, coolly, "Why, yes, I suppose I must go. That girl is quite a Messalina and would never forgive me if I disappointed her."

"Is it possible," said Cecilia, "her bold blue eyes meant something then?"

"Indeed they did," I rejoined, "and let me tell you, she is an uncommon fine girl, and quite ripe."

Nothing more passed, and after a little languid toying, for we were both tired out, we fell asleep.

The following Monday was the day appointed for me to go to Richmond, but all the way, as I rode along, I felt a vague uneasiness about Cecilia which I could not account for. There was a feverish excitement of manner about her the last few days. She was absent and abstracted, gave incoherent answers, or none at all, and was altogether quite unlike herself. What could it mean? I asked myself again and again, but at length, weary of speculation, I put spurs to my horse and galloped on.

Arrived at Richmond, I put up my horse at the Star and Garter, and enquiring my way to the Rectory (as a blind) I strolled slowly on; by and by I came to the wood which Miss Medley had so carefully described to me, and following a particular path I soon arrived at the trysting place.

Imagine my surprise when, instead of my lovely friend, I found an old gipsy woman seated under the tree. On seeing me, she rose, and dropping me a curtsey handed me a little three cornered and scented billet. I tore it open, and read these words.

"I have not been sufficiently careful with my linen; some stains have been seen and my aunt will not let me go out alone—I am in despair."

I put half-a-crown into the old woman's hand and turned on my heel. She stopped me.

"What, your honour, are you going away without an effort? Consider, sir, the young lady is over head and ears in love with you; leave the matter to me, and I will arrange it."

"Say you so, my good woman," said I, "in that case I will pay you well. You know who I am, I suppose?"

"Of course I do, your honour, all our tribe know you well, Sir Charles, for have you ever turned us off your land; have you ever taken us before the beak when we robbed your poultry yard; do you not let us sleep in your barns; and did you not send us camp blankets and provisions last winter? Oh, we know you very well, and a right noble gentleman you are. A little given to the girls, perhaps, like other fine gentlemen, but what of that? Now look you, Sir Charles, we gipsies have a mysterious way of finding out things—take a friendly hint, don't return the same way you came, go the other road, or blood may come of it."

So saying, and before I could prevent her, she dived into the wood and disappeared.

The plot thickened and I began to feel now really uncomfortable, but you know cowardice was never one of my faults; besides, I had my sword, not the toy called by that name which one wears on gala occasions but a plain, strong, serviceable weapon which had served me well in several duels; I therefore rode on the way I came, regardless of the gipsy's caution.

As I rode along the road which traverses the wood skirting my demesne, I observed a coach with imperial and portmanteaus strapped upon it, drawn up as if for concealment off the road and almost hidden amongst the trees. The coachman lay stretched on the grass while the horses grazed as they stood.

Taking no further notice of this travelling equipage I rode into the wood, and tying my horse to a tree wandered about in different directions. At length, about fifty yards from me in a small open glade, I could perceive through the trees a lady and gentleman in amorous dalliance. I approached stealthily without being seen and ensconced myself in a copse, where I had full view of all that passed, though I could not hear what was said.

On the grass lay a tall handsome dark man, who I at once recognised as Lady Cecilia's cousin, Lord William B., while lying upon the young man was her ladyship herself, her clothes thrown up, displaying all her hinder beauties which Lord B. was playfully slapping as she bounded up and down upon him.

They were evidently very much pleased with each other, and the rapturous kisses, the "oh!" and "ahs!" were the only sounds that reached me. After some time they reversed the position, he kneeling up behind her and she wriggling and bounding in the most extatic delight.

At length, their climax came. She turned round and throwing her arms round her lover's neck, they sank down quite exhausted.

In an age when the spirit of amorous intrigue pervades the court, it was not to be expected that a person of quality like Lady Cecilia would be very rigid, more especially as Lord William B. was an old flame of hers.

And remembering my own infidelities towards her I should never have taken umbrage at any she might have indulged in, had they been carried on openly as mine were. But this clandestine meeting when she thought I was gone out for the day disturbed me.

I was anxious to gather from their conversation what was the meaning of it. So soon, therefore, as they finished their first delights and were seated lovingly side by side on the grass, I crept up through the gorse and underwood till I found myself about a yard from them. Here, motionless as a statue, my hand on my sword, I listened.

"I was saying," said Lord William, "that this man must be a thorough old beast, a goat, a satyr, my dear coz, who ought never to have had you. The things you have told me, and pardi, I am no saint, really quite make my hair stand on end. Intrigue is one thing, damme, but to debauch children, fie, fie—"

"Perhaps," cried Cecilia, laughing, "he would say could he hear you, to amuse oneself with little children who are nobody's property is one thing, but to debauch another man's wife is another. Damme, fie, fie—"

Lord William laughed, but bit his lip, annoyed at the repartee.

"In fine, my dear William," said Cecilia, "it is so much easier to see the wickedness of other people's actions than our own. I'll venture to assert that if every man now living got his deserts, there would be few escape. Let fanatics abuse their fellow creatures, condemning them wholesale to hell—human nature, depend upon it, is the same everywhere, whether under a parson's cassock or soldier's scarlet coat."

"Granted, my little philosopher," laughed her cousin, "but did you not tell me that you regarded your husband with abhorrence and detestation?"

"Oh, doubtless, doubtless! Yes, he is detestable; a horrid, debauched old scoundrel, no question; but that is no reason you, who have just made him a cuckold, should add insult to injury by calling him names. How do you know that he is not nearer than we think and might suddenly—"

"Appear!" I hoarsely exclaimed springing into the open space where they were seated, sword in hand.

"To your feet, my lord; draw and defend yourself. The intrigue I could have pardoned, for it is the custom of the age in which we live; but the abuse is too insulting, and on your part, my lady, too cruel; but enough of words. Guard!"

I placed myself in fencing attitude. Lord William (who was an antagonist not to be despised, being one of the first swordsmen of the day), raised his sword to his head *en salute;* then gracefully throwing himself into the second position our blades crossed with a clashing sound that elicited a little shriek from Lady Cecilia, who sank, half fainting on the greensward.

The duel lasted some time; we were combatants worthy of each other. *Carte* and *tierce, volte,* and *demi volte,* all the finesse of fencing was tried by each for some time in vain.

At length I pricked him in the sword arm and his cambric sleeve was crimsoned in an instant. The wound only roused his anger; he lost his coolness and did not keep himself so well covered; lunging then under his *tierce* guard, I should certainly have despatched him had not the traitress, Lady Cecilia, at that instant struck up my arm with Lord William's cane; and at the same moment his sword passed through my body.

I fell back like a dead man, without sense or motion.

When I again opened my eyes, they rested on various familiar objects; I was in my private chamber. At the foot of the bed was seated Phoebe, her eyes red with weeping. I tried to speak, but she put her finger to her lip, and approaching, said, "Pray don't try yet, Sir Charles."

"What has happened?" I faintly exclaimed.

"Not now, not now," whispered Phoebe; "you shall know all about it another time. You have been light-headed and very ill, and for three days that kind young surgeon who scarcely ever left your side despaired of your life; but if you will only keep quiet, dear Sir Charles, all may yet be well."

She put a cooling drink to my lips, and shading the light moved further off. I found myself from loss of blood to be weak as a baby, so closing my eyes was soon again unconscious. In another week I was a little better, to the great delight of the poor doctor (to whom I had certainly shown many acts of kindness, never expecting such a faithful and grateful return for it). He told me that the right lung had been pierced and that the hemorrhage had at first been so great that he despaired of staunching it; but that quiet, the excellent nursing of old Jukes, Phoebe, and Chloe, who had sat up with me in turns, and an iron constitution had combined to save me. He said not a word of himself or his own skill, so that when, about a month afterwards, being convalescent, I presented him with a cheque for one hundred guineas, he regarded me with astonishment, declaring that ten was all he deserved; but I would not be gainsaid and sent him away rejoicing.

Feeling myself now well enough to hear Phoebe's recital, and kissing her and Chloe and even poor old Jukes with much ardour as I thanked them for their tender care of me, I made the two former seat themselves, at my feet, while Daphnis placed a pillow at my back and handed me a glass of lemonade.

"It is little I have to tell you, Sir Charles," began Phoebe, "but I will endeavour to be as clear as possible. Soon after your departure for Richmond, her ladyship went out alone on foot. As we had no orders to watch my lady, I would not permit Jack to do so, and we saw her no more. About five in the afternoon Jack was rambling about in the woods outside the walls when suddenly he came upon the spot where, to his great horror, you lay weltering in your blood.

"There was blood on the turf all about, which was much trampled down. You lay on your back, pale as death. Near you he picked up a fan, a ribbon, and a lady's glove; and returning to the dairy at speed he at once told us what had happened, directed us to bring your body in quietly and make up a bed in this room while he galloped off for the doctor."

"My dear boy," said I, extending him my hand, "your presence of mind and decision in all probability saved my life. I thank you, and will remember it. Go on, Phoebe."

"Well, sir, we did just as he bid us, and the doctor came; you know the rest."

"And Lady Cecilia?" I exclaimed.

"Oh," said Phoebe, "Jack must tell you all about her ladyship, for as soon as he had heard what the doctor had to say and saw you in good hands, he brought your horse, which you had left tied to a tree, into the yard, put a pair of loaded pistols into the holsters, buckled on your short sword and rode away."

"Do you, then, continue the narrative, Daphnis," said I.

The boy hesitated a moment, and then began.

"You will readily understand, Sir Charles, that being quick of apprehension, seeing you lying there with your drawn sword still in your hand, a glove, a ribbon, a fan, and the prints of strange footmarks, and those, too, from shoes not such as are generally worn by the vulgar or by highwaymen, I rapidly came to the conclusion that my lady had met a gallant in the wood, that you had surprised them, and that the duel was the consequence.

"Then I followed the footprints in the moist mossy turf,

which showed clear owing to the recent rains, until they nearly reached the road; here the marks of wheels appeared, a coach-and-four had been driven off the road and into the wood, had stopped where the footprints ended, and then skirting the wood, debouched on the road. Putting spurs to your horse's flanks, I galloped on. At the next town I heard news of the fugitives; twelve miles further on they had changed horses; at the next six miles they had supped. It was now quite dark, but still I galloped on; soon however I lost them; there were three roads in diverse directions and no one could give me a clue to the one they had taken. Horse and self being now quite worn out, I stopped at the nearest inn and retired to rest. The next morning I made the best of my way to Hastings. Here I learnt that a lady and gentleman answering their description had sailed for France five hours before."

I thanked Daphnis for his zeal, but assured him he had taken a great deal of unnecessary trouble.

I will now conclude this long story by telling you I subsequently heard that Lord William having quarrelled with a Frenchman at a public gaming table, blows ensued which resulted in a duel, and the Frenchman left his lordship stark dead on the field.

As for Lady Cecilia, broken hearted at the loss of her cousin and lover, she entered a convent of Benedictine nuns and has lately taken the black veil.

But it is time to put an end to this long letter, so, adieu!

Conclusion

To Thalia

You ask me, dear friend, where I have been hiding myself the last fifteen years. Alas! we are both that much older since we last corresponded. I was, however, about to indite a letter to you, having heard from Jack Bellsize that you had just returned from India with your husband, the General.

You duly received my communication of the affair with Lord William B., you tell me, and wrote a long letter in reply, but I never got it.

After these unfortunate events I took a disgust to my villa at Twickenham, which I sold for a good price to Sir Bulkeley H., and retreated, with Phoebe, Chloe, Daphnis and old Jukes, to my Herefordshire estate, where I have resided ever since.

As for Miss Medley, having heard from the gipsy of my intended departure she eloped one night from her aunt's and joined us. She remained with me about five years when an opportunity offering for her to make an advantageous marriage with a young farmer, I persuaded her to have him and stocked their farm for them.

To Mrs. J., I presented the house in which she lived, taking an affectionate farewell of that excellent lady. Augusta and Agnes I suitably provided for, and also found husbands for Miss Marshall and Miss Jennings, giving to each a dowry.

Poor old Jukes died five years since, come Michaelmas.

Daphnis I started in life with an ensign's commission in a marching regiment when he was about eighteen; poor lad, he fell gloriously while leading his men at a forlorn hope in storming some place in the Low Countries (not Cunnyland), such is the fortune of war; and a more gallant youth never campaigned in the fields of Venus or Mars.

Phoebe, now a fine buxom woman of thirty-five, retains all her good looks and much of her freshness. She is sweet tempered and affectionate as ever.

Chloe has grown up a lovely creature and is now twenty-eight.

Having "lived every day of my life," as the saying is, you will readily suppose that I cannot perform the feats of Venus I once indulged in, but two or three blooming little girls who pass for the sisters and cousins of Phoebe and Chloe serve to amuse me by their playfullness and tumbling about, showing their beauties, sometimes stir my sluggish blood into a thrill.

Occasionally I am able to remind Phoebe and Chloe of my old vigour and have a fucktious romp, but—"From fifty to four-score, once a week and no more."

They each have a strapping young fellow as a lover, and my consideration in this regard, so far from alienating them, only makes them more amiable and compliant to my wishes.

By my neighbours these dear girls and old friends are regarded as favourite domestics merely, a discreet old woman, the cook, who supplied old Jukes' place, playing propriety. So I am no longer a rake.

The rector of the parish is my very good friend.

My faithful surgeon lives in the house, being still a bachelor.

So, with the extra aid of two neighbouring squires, we have our bowl of punch and a rubber.

This quiet life suits me admirably, and I have forever bid adieu to the gay world and the pleasures of the town; passing much of my time in reading those philosophical writers, who are just now making such an impression on the public mind.

And now, dear friend, having given you all the news, I would fain express a hope that you will some day find your way into this remote region, but if the fates decree otherwise, then accept my farewell. *Vale! Vale! Longum Vale!*

FINIS

The Adventures of a School-Boy

The Adventures
OF
a School-Boy

OR,
THE FREAKS OF YOUTHFUL PASSION.

The tender spring upon thy tempting lip
  Shows thee unripe, yet may'st thou well be tasted.
Make use of time; let not advantage slip.
  Beauty within itself should not be wasted.
Fairflowers that are not gathered in their prime,
  Rot and consume themselves in little time.
                                    SHAKESPEARE.

LONDON:
PRINTED FOR THE BOOKSELLERS.
MDCCCLXVI.

[Title page of original edition]

A Note to This Edition

The Adventures of a School-Boy was published in London in 1866 and carried this Preface by the publisher:

The following pages, as will be observed from the allusions contained in them, are only a portion of the autobiography of a gentleman who has probably gone through more amorous adventures than most of his contemporaries. The first part of the manuscript in the hands of the editor contains the details of his having been left an orphan at the age of fourteen the heir to a large fortune, of his having been sent to school, and of his first initiation into the mysteries of pleasure. But this part, though interesting to a certain class of readers, may perhaps not be so generally acceptable to the public; the editor has therefore selected a portion, which, he hopes, will be found agreeable to all. It will depend upon the manner in which the present work is received whether any other portion of the manuscript shall see the light.

Henry Ashbee, in *Index Librorum Prohibitorum,* mentions that the original edition contained eight colored lithographs, "badly drawn and executed," which were designed by Edward Sellon, the author of *The New Epi-*

curean. Ashbee goes on to say that *The Adventures of a School-Boy*

> ... is by no means badly written, and is from the pen of one well versed in the art of composition; the author's name must for the present remain a secret, the narrative is not without interest, and the scenes are natural and lascivious. Dugdale thus catalogues it: "A very natural and powerfully written tale, describing in vivid colours the seduction of two young and delicious creatures by two sprigs of fashion, Eaton [sic] scholars, and the gradual transition from the most refined voluptuousness to the grossest sensuality are [sic] richly and lusciously depicted."

The Adventures of a School-Boy

Among all my school-fellows, there was no one to whom, especially after the departure of Hamilton, I felt so much attached as George Vivian. Several circumstances contributed to cement our intimacy, and we had not been long acquainted before we were on such a footing as to have no secrets from one another. I have already adverted to the favourable impression which his conduct towards me on the occasion of the flogging had produced upon my mind, and I was very desirous to do anything in my power to show him how much I had felt it.

He, too, was an orphan like myself, and having likewise been brought up almost entirely among ladies, he could enter into all my feelings better than most of our school-fellows, who had been accustomed to the amusements and sports of large families. In one respect he had at first an advantage of me, for though he had only been for a short time at the Doctor's he had previously been for a year at another school and, of course, was more up to the ways of school-boys than I was. He was clever and quick and had a most excellent memory, but unfortunately the school he had been at formerly was not well conducted and his teachers had been quite satisfied that he could repeat the lesson set him, without taking the trouble to ascertain whether he understood it or not. His natural cleverness enabled him to keep his place with most of his school-fellows at the Doctor's, but it was not long before I discovered my own superiority. I was quite convinced that if he chose to exert himself he could stand much higher in the school than he did. In most things where memory and quickness availed, he was not behind anyone, but what he failed in was where it was necessary to apply to some purpose the rules which he had no difficulty in learning by heart, but of which it could hardly be said he knew the meaning. Above all things he felt his deficiency in the capacity of making verses, and he was constantly obliged to apply to some of his companions for assistance. After a short time, I was his principal resource, and though I would sometimes scold him for not trying to do them himself, I always cheerfully gave him all the assistance in my power.

One day, however, I asked him seriously whether he would not feel much happier if he could depend upon himself rather than be obliged to have recourse always to another for assistance. He was somewhat annoyed at first, and said that if I grudged the trouble he would not apply to me again.

I said it was not at all the trouble I thought of, as he knew quite well it was no trouble to me, but that I considered that with his abilities he might very easily learn to do them much better than I could, and that what I wanted to persuade him to do would, for a time at least, give me a great deal more trouble than making the verses myself.

He said it was no use to think of it, as he had often tried but never could succeed, though he admitted that he felt greatly annoyed at his inferiority in this respect to others who were greatly below him in most subjects.

I at length persuaded him to allow me to attempt to explain to him the rules, which he could repeat but the meaning and application of which he had never thoroughly understood, and he agreed to devote a certain time every day to this purpose. It was at first rather a hard struggle as it obliged us for a time to abandon some of our amusements, and he was several times on the point of giving up the attempt. In the course of a few weeks, however, he began to have a glimpse of what I wanted to impress upon him, and thenceforward he was as anxious as I could be to prosecute our private studies. It seemed to come upon him like a flash of lightning, and he could not imagine, when he first began to see the light, how it was that he had remained so long in the dark.

The change in him was so great that it attracted the attention of the Doctor, who had not previously done justice to his abilities; his commendations not only gratified George, but encouraged him to exert himself still more.

His gratitude to me for having thus drawn forth his powers and made him conscious of his own abilities was extreme, and there was nothing he would not have done to convince me how strong this feeling was.

We used often to talk about our previous histories and compare our thoughts and feelings. He had lost his parents at an early age, and had been brought up by his grandmother—a stern, though not unkind old lady. She resided in a curious old mansion which had formerly been an Abbey, and the only inmates of the family were a maiden daughter, approaching fifty years of age, and two young ladies, one a year and the other a few months younger than George.

These young ladies were not related to him, being

relatives of his grandmother's second husband. They were both well provided for, but being without any near relations they had lived under the charge of his grandmother as long as he could recollect.

Of these girls he would never tire of speaking, and he soon gave me the details of everything that had passed with them. He had no companions of his own sex, and his whole time was spent with them. They shared the lessons in Greek and Latin which he received from the curate of the parish, and he, in turn, participated in their French, Italian, music, and dancing lessons, for which masters attended from a neighbouring town.

Their schoolroom was a large apartment, somewhat detached from the house, which had formerly been the chapel of the Abbey. As from its situation any noise they made there did not disturb the inhabitants of the rest of the house, this apartment gradually came to be their usual resort and the scene of all their indoor amusements. The greater part of the walls were covered with book presses, which were kept locked and from which they occasionally persuaded their aunt to allow them to take a few books, such as she approved of. As they grew older, however, and became fond of reading, they longed to become better acquainted with the contents of the bookshelves.

Luckily George discovered a key which opened the presses and enabled them to gratify their curiosity. For some time they indulged themselves, to their great delight, with the perusal of *Tom Jones, Peregrine Pickle,* and some other works of the old school which had been carefully concealed from them, but with which they were highly diverted.

One day they made a discovery which, at first, startled them not a little. While replacing some books on an upper shelf, George allowed one to get behind the others, and leaning forward to pick it up, his foot slipped, and he nearly fell from the chair. This made him press forcibly against the bookshelf, and in doing so he touched a secret spring, upon which the shelf started forward and disclosed a small recess behind.

Their curiosity was of course excited to ascertain what the hiding place contained, and they discovered two or three old books, which, from the dust on them, had evidently not been touched for many years. They turned out on inspection to be some collections of erotic plates, from the Académie des Dames, Aretino, and other works of a similar description.

Their astonishment on seeing these may be imagined; George was delighted with them, and attracted by the sight of the naked figures and the strange attitudes, he wished to examine them minutely; but the girls said they were not proper to be looked at, and insisted on putting them back. George, however, was not satisfied with this hasty glance, but used often to return to them by himself and pore over them, wondering what their meaning could be.

Before long, too, he became aware, from noticing that the position of the books was sometimes changed that, though the girls had professed to him their dislike to look at them, they also were in the habit of amusing themselves with them in secret. To make certain of this, he one day concealed himself beneath the sofa, and when he found them employed in examining the plates, he made his appearance and, somewhat to their confusion, rallied them upon their pretended modesty, which he now found was no greater safeguard against their curiosity than his own.

After this there could be no further disguise on the

subject amongst them, and they used often to take the books down, examine the pictures, and discuss their different ideas and conjectures as to the purposes and meanings of the various attitudes. This led before long to a comparison between the beauties of the figures thus represented, and those of the similar parts which they themselves possessed. George vowed that he was certain the girls were much handsomer than any of the personages represented on the plates, and insisted on satisfying himself on the point, but they at first resisted his attempts to gratify this very natural curiosity.

One day, when they were discussing the strange appearance of the virile member as represented in a state of erection, George took courage and, letting down his trousers, exhibited to them his little bijou, with all its surrounding attributes, that they might compare it with the representation.

They pretended at first to be shocked, but curiosity and desire soon got the better of every other feeling, so that, after he had induced them to explore all his secret charms, he had not much difficulty in persuading them to gratify him by exposing in turn all the beauties they had to show.

The ice having been once broken, this soon became their constant amusement when they had a safe opportunity for indulging in it. But at this time they were all too young to be able to comprehend, and still less to put in practice, the lessons which were thus exhibited to them.

In imitation of the scenes depicted in the plates, George would get between their thighs and endeavour to introduce his little member, which their caresses had made quite stiff, within their secret recesses; but as the attempt to insert it always occasioned pain to them, and was not accompanied by any corresponding increase of pleasure to

George, they soon gave up attempting what appeared to them to be something preposterous, and contented themselves with toying with and kissing and caressing each other's secret charms.

At first the total absence of hair from the parts of their own bodies, which they saw depicted in the engravings as surrounded with curly locks, occasioned them some amazement; but in the course of time it became evident that Eliza, the elder of the cousins, was beginning to give proof positive that this was not an exaggeration of the artist, as they had at first supposed. Her bubbies too began to swell out, and her mount to increase in size, and George found that when he tickled and played with her little secret part, she now exhibited more evident tokens of pleasure and enjoyment.

His own pretty jewel too was now becoming more and more excited, and was increasing considerably in size, while the two little appendages began to show themselves more prominently depending from the belly, and hanging down as he saw them represented in the pictures.

In short, matters were fast progressing in the natural train, so as to bring on with them the age of puberty, and a very short time longer would no doubt have sufficed not only to render them capable, but to supply the desires which would induce them to carry their experiments far enough to initiate them into the whole secret; but to their infinite sorrow and regret, their pleasant party was suddenly dispersed.

George's grandmother, Mrs. Montague, had another daughter who had been for some time residing abroad. She had recently been attacked with a dangerous illness, which threatened to be of long continuance; and at her urgent request, Mrs. Montague had been induced to break up her establishment at the Abbey, and proceed with her unmarried daughter to join the invalid in Italy.

This, of course, involved a complete separation between George and his fair companions. After a sorrowful parting, the girls went to a boarding school, and George was also sent to a school, where he was so uncomfortable that at length he petitioned to be removed. To his great joy this was agreed to; and he went to the Doctor's, where he had only been for a few months when I joined him.

When we became intimate, nothing rejoiced him so much as to talk of the girls, and many a long conversation we had regarding them, when he would detail to me all the minute particulars of what had passed between them, and bitterly regret his own ignorance and want of ability to avail himself of the pleasure which he now thought he might have enjoyed; and he looked forward with the greatest eagerness to the enjoyment he anticipated when he should again have the happiness of meeting them.

One day after I had been for some time at school, he came to me in great delight, with an open letter in his hand which he told me to read. It was from his grandmother, who a short time previously had returned to the Abbey, and contained an invitation for him to spend the summer holidays with her. She mentioned that he would meet his old friends Eliza and Maria, who had again come to reside with her, and told him that if he wished he might bring one of his school-fellows with him as a companion. His object was now to induce me to accompany him on this visit, and to participate with him in all the enjoyments he anticipated on meeting his two old friends.

Although I was by no means quite so sanguine as he was of our being at once admitted to all his previous intimacy, still I was very anxious to see the girls of whom I had heard so much, and readily agreed to his proposal, thinking that what had previously happened gave us a fair reason to hope that even all his anticipations might be realized.

Accordingly, on the appointed day, having made ourselves as smart as possible, we arrived at the Abbey. It was near the dinner hour when we reached it, and we were received by his grandmother—a stately though by no means disagreeable dame—who told us that we had just time to get ready for dinner.

We proceeded to decorate ourselves as quickly as possible; and like young fools, as we then were, we fancied that we would be most likely to make an impression by affecting as much as possible the appearance and manners of the man. When we met the family party in the drawing room, I was greatly struck with the beauty of the two girls, and could not help acknowledging that the glowing description George had so often given of them was by no means an exaggeration of the reality.

The impression made upon me by our reception was of the most favourable description; but with poor George it was quite the reverse. Being an utter stranger I could expect nothing beyond civility, and I was not at all surprised at the coldness with which the girls received me. George, whose impressions of their former intimacy were just as vivid as if they had only separated the day previously, had calculated upon being received exactly on the same footing as that on which they had parted. And on going up to them with open arms, he was horrified to find that he was received upon the same cold and frigid terms which were accorded to me.

He was sadly mortified at this cool treatment and at

finding that all his advances were met with the utmost reserve, while he was addressed as Mr. George and I as Sir Francis, on every occasion.

Poor George could not conceal his mortification, and with difficulty prevented the tears from gushing from his eyes at the sad contrast which this reception presented to the delightful interview he had pictured to himself. I, of course, had never anticipated anything else so far as I was concerned but I was more at my ease, and consequently able to observe matters more calmly. It struck me that there was something forced and overdone in the manner in which the girls were acting; and that it looked rather as if they were afraid of themselves and were obliged to resort to all this formality to prevent their showing their real feelings.

While, therefore, I was polite and attentive to them, I devoted myself almost exclusively to the old ladies, upon whom I was desirous to produce a good impression, directing my conversations chiefly to them and avoiding in this manner any appearance of being too anxious to make myself agreeable to the young ladies.

In this way I was enabled to make my observations on their demeanour more easily and without attracting attention. As the evening wore on, matters did not improve so far as George was concerned. The same cold and formal stiffness was still kept up towards him. Once, when we were left alone with the young ladies he summoned up courage, and on some pretext took an opportunity of passing his arm round Maria's waist, but he was instantly met with a sharp "Come, come, behave yourself, sir; we must not have any of your school-boy tricks here."

Poor George was quite abashed at such an unexpected rejoinder, and hardly ventured to open his mouth again during the evening. I, however, rattled away as well as I could, and did my best to amuse the old ladies, and make things pass off pleasantly.

At George's suggestion we had been accommodated in two adjoining apartments, which he had formerly occupied, and which were situated in a semidetached wing abutting on the library.

When we had retired to our rooms for the night, George was quite frantic at the manner in which he had been treated, and was half inclined to be angry with me for taking the matter so coolly as I did; and now, when he could freely give way to his feelings, the tears which he had hitherto had some difficulty in suppressing rolled down his cheeks. I had been disposed to rally him a little on his disappointment, but when I saw how seriously he took it to heart, I had not the cruelty to add to his annoyance, and proceeded to try to console him a little. I reminded him that now more than two years had elapsed since he and his fair friends had met.

During that period he had acquired a good deal of experience and knowledge of the world, and it was only reasonable to suppose that the girls also must have made similar progress. That during all this time they had had no opportunity of ascertaining what his views and feelings were, beyond the exchange of a few formal letters which were necessarily very guarded on both sides; and that it was hardly reasonable to expect that they should at once throw themselves into his arms—a proceeding which they might naturally suppose would appear to him more like the conduct of two prostitutes than anything else, and more likely to disgust him than otherwise.

He admitted that there was some truth in this, and that he had expected too much at first. But he was much more relieved when I proceeded to tell him the opinion I had formed, that in their conduct this evening the girls were only acting a part. I related to him some observations I had made, which led me to think that my first supposition to this effect was correct.

What chiefly satisfied him was one circumstance I had remarked while I was playing chess with Miss Vivian, and they thought I was not observing them. George was standing opposite us, looking over a portfolio of engravings which his grandmother had brought from the Continent. While turning them over he raised his foot upon a chair to support the portfolio, the light was shining strong upon his figure, and the proportions of his manly appendage were plainly exhibited.

Poor George was thinking less of the engravings he was turning over, than of those he had been accustomed in former days to amuse himself with, along with his fair companions, and this caused the unruly member to be in rather an excited state. Its full development attracted the attention of Maria, who, with a smile, pointed it out to Eliza, and a meaningful look passed between them as if they were well pleased to see such a change upon it.

All this byplay did not escape my observation, though they thought I was too intent on my game to observe it, and from George's position he could not be at all conscious that he was the object of their attention.

What I thus told George comforted him very much, and with some anxiety he asked my advice as to what we ought to do in the circumstances in which we found ourselves, so different from what he had expected. I told him I was afraid we had made a sad mistake in trying, as we had done, to play the young gentlemen, and that we had thereby given them too good an opportunity of keeping us at a distance, which they would hardly have been able to do if we had come down upon them in the character of two riotous school-boys. I said that it was perhaps not yet too late to rectify the error, and that as Miss Maria had chosen to refer to school-boy tricks, it was worth while to try, at least, whether we could not play some upon them to good effect. He said he was willing to do anything I thought best, as nothing could be more unsatisfactory than our present position. We therefore determined on our course, and after consoling one another in the best way we could for our present disappointment, we fell asleep.

The next morning, discarding broadcloth and silks, jewellery and French polish, we made our appearance at breakfast in short jackets, trousers of plain woolen stuff, fitting close to our waist and haunches, open breasted waist coats, and our necks merely encircled with a light handkerchief loosely tied in front. I cannot so well say what this effect had upon myself, though I had no reason to suppose from George's compliments on my appearance that it was unfavourable. But in so far as he was concerned, I could not help thinking that it was a great improvement, and that he now looked to be much more likely to captivate a girl's fancy than he had appeared to be on the previous evening, when dressed up to the highest pitch of the then youthful fashion. Like myself he had rather a young appearance for his age. This suited our purpose well, and I had little doubt we should be able to pass ourselves off in the character we had assumed.

Perhaps a close observer would have remarked that our forms were more rounded, and our muscles more prominent than was reconcilable with our assumed youthful appearance; but this was not likely to be much noticed in the quarter where alone we cared about making a good impression. Our only fear was that our thin, tight-fitting trousers might betray to the elder ladies the secret of our manly organs having arrived at a size and proportion likely to render us dangerous companions for two young girls.

But we resolved to be cautious in our movements and proceedings before them, for there had been an object in our purposely selecting these garments—in order that without appearing to make any display, we might have an opportunity of exhibiting to the young ladies, as if accidentally, on every possible occasion that there was something beneath them which was likely to prove an agreeable and satisfactory plaything, if they would only throw off their reserve and give us an excuse for producing them for their amusement.

During breakfast, George and I talked of nothing but the sporting amusements which we looked forward to enjoying in the country; and as soon as the meal was over he insisted on carrying me off to the river to fish, where we remained all day till dinner time.

I thought I observed some slight indications of disappointment at our course of procedure; but as this was exactly what we wished, we were encouraged to pursue our plan.

During the evening I devoted myself as before, almost exclusively to the old ladies; and George, who had somewhat recovered his spirits, amused himself with occasionally teasing the younger ones a little, at the same time taking every opportunity he could find of allowing them, as if accidentally, to catch a glimpse of the proportions of a certain weapon, which he eagerly longed to make use of, and which every now and then he made to erect itself and, as if unconsciously on his part, to appear prominently beneath his trousers.

On more than one occasion, when he contrived to do this in such a position that they thought he could not observe them, I noticed the same meaningful look of satisfaction pass between the girls which I had observed the previous evening. Upon the whole, we were convinced that everything was now proceeding as satisfactorily as we could expect.

The next morning at breakfast we continued the same game, and George again proposed some expedition which would occupy the whole day; but here his grandmother interfered and said, "Come, come, George, this will never do. You must not engross Sir Francis so entirely, you see enough of him at school, and you must allow us to have a little of his company while he is here. Why, here are the two young ladies who have been putting off any distant excursion all the summer, until they should have somebody to escort them about."

George and I exchanged a quiet look of satisfaction at this exposé, and at once said that if the ladies would accept of our services, we were quite at their command whenever they chose.

They, on their part, disclaimed any wish to interfere with our amusements, but Mrs. Montague again struck in and said, "Well, George, you and Sir Francis can occupy yourselves in any way you like till lunch time. After that I shall order the horses to be at the door, and you can take him to see the old castle. If you have forgot the way, the ladies will be able to show it to you."

After lunch we accordingly set off on an expedition to some ruins about ten miles off. As it was by no means our plan to remain on a distant footing with our friends, when we had them by themselves we both endeavoured by all means in our power, when thus thrown into close contact with them, to make ourselves as agreeable as possible.

Before long we separated into two pairs, George taking Maria who was just of his own age, and leaving Eliza for me. I believe we both at first took the same mode of proceeding—that of praising each other, being pretty well assured that what we said of one another would not fail to be repeated by the listener to her friend.

I soon found myself rapidly improving my intimacy with Eliza, who was not only an extremely handsome, but an accomplished girl; and I strove, not without some success, to make myself as agreeable as possible to her, though of course I at first preserved the utmost respect in my manner, so as not to alarm her.

When we reached the ruins we put up our horses and walked about, in order to inspect them thoroughly. George and Maria soon separated from us. Eliza sat down to take a sketch of the ruins, and after sitting talking to her for a while, I also drew out my sketchbook, and took up my position a little behind her, imitating her example.

While thus occupied, I could occasionally hear from the merry tones they made use of that George and Maria were getting on at a most satisfactory rate. At length, when I had nearly completed my sketch, and was filling in the foreground with the outline of Eliza's figure, they came up behind us, and looking over my shoulder, Maria exclaimed, "Oh, Sir Francis, how beautiful that is! I should so like to have it, it is such a capital likeness of Eliza. Oh, pray, do give it to me."

I answered, "By all means! But upon one condition, and that is that you will persuade Miss Eliza to give me in exchange her sketch, as a remembrance of the place."

Having heard what passed, Eliza now turned round to us, and on looking at my drawing, she said that Maria might do anything she liked with hers as it was not good for anything, and she would make a much better one by copying mine. The exchange was accordingly made.

Seeing that there were some other sketches in my book, they asked to be allowed to look at them. I appeared to hesitate and said that I was not quite sure I could permit this, that they must recollect a school-boy's sketchbook was generally filled with everything that came in his way which struck his fancy, sometimes without much regard to propriety.

In fact, the very reason why I had selected this book was that among other things, it contained several sketches of George and myself, taken when we were bathing, and exhibiting our naked figures at full length. There was nothing absolutely indecent in them, either in the attitudes or even in the form and position of the Priapean member, but there was no attempt to conceal it, and it was exhibited in its full natural proportions when in a state of rest, with its shading of foliage, as yet but scanty, around it. My hesitation only excited their curiosity the more; and though Eliza said little, Maria pressed me to show them anything I thought I could.

I then turned over the leaves, allowing them to look at some of the other sketches, and when I came to those of ourselves, I at first folded down part of the leaf and only exhibited the upper portion of our persons naked as far as the navel.

Though they made no observation, I saw from their flushed cheeks how much they were affected by the sight; and when they came to one or two sketches where our virile members were not so prominently displayed, although sufficiently indicated, I allowed them to see them, affecting to do so through awkwardness in turning over the leaves. When they had gone over the whole they expressed their admiration and their thanks; and we soon after mounted our horses to return home.

While getting the horses out, George found an opportunity to tell me what I had already guessed from the expression on his face, that he had got on even better than he had expected with Maria. That though she would not allow him to take any serious liberty, he thought this arose more from the fear of being observed than from unwillingness on her part; and he had even been able more than once to place his hand upon his old darling friend, now clothed in a new dress; and had made her grasp and feel the increased proportions of his throbbing weapon.

This was as much as we could possibly expect and emboldened by what he told me, I ventured while raising Eliza into the saddle and adjusting her dress, to press her leg and bottom, and even to insinuate my hand under the riding habit and touch the naked, soft, smooth skin of her thigh, without meeting with either rebuke or resistance.

We had a merry ride home, and during dinner all were in high spirits. George, especially, was so much so that it attracted the observation of his grandmother, who made some remark upon it; to which he replied that he had formerly been so scolded for being a madcap, that he had been trying for the last two days to see if he could not gain a better character, but that he found it was of no use to make the attempt, and he must just submit to the reproach.

This produced a smile, and the evening passed on very pleasantly. For the first time since our arrival, the piano was opened, and the young ladies gave us some music. They both had good voices, and sang well; but they wanted that taste and polish which can only be acquired by hearing first-rate performers. I had had great advantages in that way in consequence of my mother's fondness for music, which was almost the only amusement she ever indulged in. During our visits to London, she was not only a regular attendant at the Opera, but was in the constant habit of having at her house all the highest talent of musical celebrity. George, too, had one of the finest voices I have ever heard, and latterly, at least, he had had the advantage of a most excellent master.

I was engaged with Miss Vivian in a game of chess, when I heard Maria say to George, "Well, George, I suppose you have entirely forgotten all the lessons in music I used to take so much pains to give you."

George laughed, but I answered for him, "No, indeed, Miss Maria, I can assure you he has not at all forgotten them, and I am quite sure you will find you have no reason to be ashamed of your pupil."

She insisted that from the way in which I spoke, I must be musical myself, and that she must get me to sing to her, as she was sure I was a much better performer than George. I replied that I would not at all deny that I was fond of music, and would be glad to do anything I could to contribute to their amusement, more especially as I saw it was useless to struggle any longer with Miss Vivian, who was just about to checkmate me, but that I must make one condition, which was that I was to be allowed to make my exhibition first, as I was quite sure that after they had heard George they would never have patience to listen to me.

I had by this time learned that it was sometimes politic

to allow one's self to be occasionally beaten, even at chess, and I very soon allowed Miss Vivian to win the game, and then joined the musical party.

I selected a song that had Eliza's name upon it. Maria smiled, and called to Eliza that it was one of her songs and she must come and play it, which she accordingly did. I tried to do my best, and certainly had no reason to be dissatisfied with the commendations which I received and, at their request, I gave them two or three more, which they suggested. I then resigned my place to George.

Maria offered to play for him, but he said he would rather accompany himself, and took his seat at the piano. He played the prelude to the beautiful air "Una furtiva Lagrima," and then commenced to sing. For the first few notes his voice rather wavered, but he soon regained his confidence, and poured out a strain of exquisite music in the most charming manner. Even I, who had been in the constant habit of hearing him sing, was surprised at the manner in which he acquitted himself, but animated by the presence of those he loved, he was evidently induced to exert himself to the utmost, and certainly he did succeed in creating a most powerful sensation. Long before he had finished, there was not a dry eye in the room. Even Mrs. Montague, usually so impassive, was roused from her imposing gravity. She first laid down her book to listen, and then rose from her seat and came and stood behind George.

When he had finished, there was perfect silence for a minute or two, and then his grandmother, who was the first to recover herself, said, "George, my dear boy, I knew you had a fine voice, but I had no idea it would have improved so greatly. You must have practised a great deal to have become so perfect. I hope it has not been at the expense of your other studies."

I here struck in, "No, indeed, Mrs. Montague. I can assure you that it has not, and I am certain if you apply to the Doctor, he will tell you the same thing. I know some people think a taste for music is a dangerous one and likely to lead one into bad society, and it may be so with some, but I am quite sure it has had quite a different effect with us; it has often amused us, and kept us out of company where we might not have been so well employed."

"I am very glad to hear it," she replied, "and I hope this will always be the case. But where did you contrive to improve yourself so much, George? I was not aware you had taken lessons in music."

"Why," answered George, "my two first instructors, to whom I owe most, are both present."

"Indeed," said I, "you owe everything to Miss Maria. At one time, I certainly had the presumption to fancy I could give you some instruction, but I soon found that the pupil was far before the master, though I suspect that neither of us would have made much progress latterly, had it not been for the kindness of the worthy signor."

"And pray who is the signor?" asked Maria.

"Why, he is an Italian nobleman—a refugee, whose acquaintance I made some time ago. His story is too long to detail here, though I shall give it you some day for it is a very curious one; but he considered he was under some obligation to me for getting my uncle to use his interest with some influential people in his favour, so as to save the remnant of his property, and he took a great fancy to George, which has induced him to devote a good deal of time and trouble to our instruction."

George was then requested to give them another song, which he did at once, and we continued the musical entertainment during the evening, taking care to make the young ladies join with us, so as to avoid any appearance of wishing to show off.

At the end of one of George's songs, I heard Maria say in a low tone, "Oh, George! George! How could you be here for two whole days without giving us this pleasure?"

"It is all your own fault," retorted he. "You snubbed me so much the first night I came, that I have been afraid ever since even to open my mouth."

When we retired to bed in the evening we congratulated ourselves on the success of our plan, feeling satisfied that we had made as much progress as we could have expected under the circumstances. In the morning, too, we had another proof of the effect we had produced on the girls. On returning from our ride the previous afternoon, I had pretended to hide my sketchbook in the pocket of my overcoat, which was hanging up in the hall, taking care that Maria should see where I put it. On looking at it in the morning, we found that it was not only quite apparent that it had been inspected, but that two of the sketches —those which gave the most complete and perfect representations of our organs of manhood—were wanting, and had evidently been cut out by our young friends. As a good many other pages had been taken out in the same manner, they probably thought the theft would never have been discovered, but I knew quite well what was there, and could not be mistaken on the subject.

We of course took no notice of this, but we thought it was a complete demonstration of their inclinations, and we determined that we should now take the first opportunity in our power to bring them to such terms as would enable us to procure the pleasure we desired to share with them.

The day turned out to be very wet, and we made an excuse of this to remain in the house and cultivate our intimacy with the girls. After breakfast, Maria said, "Well, George, will you come to the drawing room, and pay me back some of the music lessons I used to give you?"

"With all my heart," said George, "there is nothing would give me greater pleasure than to practise *all* the lessons you used to teach me."

She blushed and seemed a little confused, but immediately led the way to the drawing room, where we spent a couple of hours practising over all the old songs they had been accustomed to sing together. At last I said, "Why, George, this will never do. If we continue at this rate we shall exhaust all our stores, and shall never be able to create a sensation again."

George, however, did not seem disposed to leave the piano, apparently thinking that his position, bending over Maria, gave him a favourable opportunity for a little fingering upon a still more delicate instrument than the one she was performing upon.

I wished to leave the field there clear for him and therefore turned to Eliza, who was sitting with her back turned to them, netting a purse.

"Oh, this is exactly what I wanted," said I. "I want to make a landing net, but I am afraid I have quite forgotten how to form the meshes. Perhaps you will be good enough to give me a lesson."

She at once assented. I brought my materials and sat down beside her. She soon discovered that I knew quite as much on the subject as she did, but she said nothing, and continued to give me all the instruction I applied for, apparently not objecting to the use I made of the opportunity afforded me of pressing her hand and taking a few other liberties with her person.

In the meantime I kept up the conversation, which soon turned upon the subject of the Abbey. I said I felt myself quite at home there and could hardly persuade myself that I had entered it for the first time only three days before; I told her that George had been so fond of talking of it, and of describing everything that had occurred to him in it, that I believed I was almost as well acquainted with it as himself, for I was quite sure there was not a room in the house he had been in, not a book he had read, not a picture he had looked at, which he had not described over and over again.

As I said this in rather a marked tone, I saw Eliza's cheeks become suffused with a deep blush, and heard Maria whisper to George, "Oh, George! George! How could you?"

"Never do you mind," was his reply. "He is quite safe: you need not be afraid of him."

I took no notice of this, and soon changed the subject, adverting to our school days, and to all we had done for one another. Among other things I told them the only time we had ever got into a regular scrape was because we had refused to tell upon each other, and preferred to submit to a flogging rather than bring each other into disgrace.

At the mention of flogging they seemed greatly interested, and Maria especially pricked up her ears and put some questions on the subject as to how often we had been subjected to it and how we liked it. Seeing that they were amused with what I told them, I continued, greatly to George's diversion, to entertain them with sundry accounts of floggings, some of which were purely imaginary and the others improvements upon scenes that had actually occurred, not with ourselves, but with some of our acquaintances.

I gradually wound up their curiosity to a high pitch and Maria especially seemed to take a great interest in the subject. Observing this, I went on to say that it was a matter which one could convey no adequate idea of by mere description, and that to understand it properly it was necessary to have gone through it, or at least to have witnessed the operation itself. "I only wish," said I, "that I had you at school some day when it was going on, that you might see the thing regularly carried through."

Maria here burst out with "Oh! it would be so funny to see it."

"Well," said I, "I am afraid there is no possibility of conveying you to school for that purpose, but here is George, who is such a perfect ladies' man, that I am quite sure if he thought it would afford you any amusement he would at once submit to undergo the operation, in order merely to give you an idea of how it is done, and for my part, I shall be quite willing to act the part of the school-master, and apply the birch in a satisfactory manner."

"Speak for yourself," said George, "I am not a bit fonder of it than you are."

The girls burst out in a fit of laughter, and I gave George a look which he at once understood as a hint to keep up the joke. I continued to banter him, alleging that he was afraid of the pain and that he had not courage enough to stand the punishment.

Maria chimed in, and encouraged me to go on. After

some little jesting on the subject, George appeared to come round, and at length agreed that he would submit to go through the ceremony of being flogged in their presence, exactly as the operation would be performed at school. He said the only thing he did not like about the punishment was the being kept in suspense, and he therefore stipulated that there should be no delay, and that the affair should be brought to a conclusion at once. I said there was but one objection to this, which was that as the punishment was to be bona fide and not in joke, there was a risk that he might make an outcry which would disturb the house and get us into a scrape.

He affected to take this in high dudgeon, and to be greatly offended at the idea that he would cry out for such a trifle, and made an excuse of it for insisting that the affair should go on, in order to prove that he did not care in the least for the pain. At length he said that if we had any apprehension on this account it might easily be obviated by our going to the old schoolroom, where any noise that might be made could not be heard in the rest of the house.

At this allusion to the schoolroom, the girls exchanged a glance of alarm, and I hastened to remove any suspicion by saying it would be better to delay until the weather improved, when the scene could take place in the open air, at a distance from the house. George, however, insisted that there should be no delay, and at length a compromise was made by which it was arranged that if the rain ceased after luncheon we should go out to the park, and if not, the ceremony should take place in the schoolroom.

As the day wore on without any symptom of improvement, George and I made all the necessary preparations. After lunch, we sat for some time with the girls without referring to the subject, which occupied all our thoughts. At length Maria made an allusion to it, upon which George started up and insisted on its being got over at once.

The so-called schoolroom—or rather library—was a large oblong apartment, which had formerly been the chapel of the Abbey. At one end was the principal entrance, and at the other a large bay window, which occupied the whole of that end of the room, with the exception of a closet on each side. The portion within the recess was elevated by two steps from the rest of the floor, and the window, though on the ground floor, was thus so high that no one on the outside could look into the room without getting up on the window sill, which, though not impossible, as George and I had already ascertained, was not an easy matter without some assistance. In the centre of the room was a long library table. A great portion of one side was taken up with a large fireplace; the remainder, and the whole of the opposite side, was occupied by bookshelves, while beside the table and opposite the fireplace, was a large old-fashioned sofa, more like a bed than a sofa of modern times.

When we reached the room I at once took upon myself the character of schoolmaster, and George assumed that of the pert school-boy. I placed the girls on the sofa, and drew a large stand for holding maps across the space between the sofa and the table, thus cutting off the communication between them and the door.

I then told George to prepare for punishment. He inquired, in a flippant tone, if he was to strip entirely naked. I pretended to be shocked, and answered with a serious air, "No, sir; you know quite well that if I were about to punish you in a severe manner I should not expose you before your companions; but take care, sir, and do not provoke me too far; for though kissing a pretty girl is a grave fault and deserves the punishment you are about to undergo, still, disrespect to your master is a much greater crime, and if you continue to show it in this manner, I shall be obliged, however unwillingly, to resort to the severest punishment in my power to inflict."

I then made him take off his coat and waistcoat, and pretended to fasten his hands above his head to the roller from which the maps depended. I then turned his handsome bottom to the girls, and taking up a birch rod which I had provided, I affected to flog his posteriors severely. He writhed and twisted his body in the most ridiculous manner, as if he was suffering greatly from the infliction of the blows, but at the same time he turned round his head, made wry faces, put out his tongue, and made fun to the girls, who were in fits of laughter and heartily enjoying the whole scene.

I rebuked him for his improper conduct, and told him that if it was continued, I must resort to severer measures with him. The more I appeared to get angry, the more he made game of me and the more outrageous he became. At length I approached him, and took hold of one hand, as if for the purpose of restraining his antics, and making him keep still, in order that I might be the better able to apply the rod; but my object was of a totally different nature. I had taken care that he should have no braces on, and his trousers were merely fastened in front by two or three buttons. These I secretly unloosened, and having satisfied myself that his beautiful organ of manhood was in a sufficiently imposing state for the exhibition I meditated, I suddenly slipped down his trousers, raised up his shirt and inflicted two or three sharp blows on his naked posteriors, pure and white as snow, saying, "There, sir, since you will have it in this manner, how do you like it so?"

I had no sooner finished than he turned round, and as I took good care to hold his shirt well up, he exhibited to the astonished eyes of the two girls an object which they have often contemplated before, but certainly never in such a beautiful or satisfactory state. There it stood bolt upright, issuing from the tender curls which had begun to adorn it, with the curious little balls, as yet unshaded with hair, but of a slightly darker colour than the rest of his person, which made them show off in contrast with the pure white of his thighs, the pillar rearing itself proudly up towards his navel, surmounted with its lovely coral head.

The whole proceeding only occupied a few seconds, and took the girls entirely by surprise. Uttering a shriek, they started up, and endeavoured to reach the door. This movement, however, had been foreseen, and as in order to arrive at it they had to go round the table, George was enabled to reach it before them. He hastily locked it, took out the key, and then planted himself before it, with his shirt tucked up round his waist, and his trousers down to his knees, exhibiting his flaming priapus as a formidable bar to their exit, while he exclaimed, "No, no! You shan't escape in this manner. You have all had your share in the amusement, and it is now my turn to have mine, and not one of you shall leave the room till you have all undergone the same punishment as I have been subjected to. Come, Frank, this is all your doing, so I must begin with you."

"By all means," replied I, "it shall never be said that I proposed to any one else what I was afraid to undergo myself."

Prepared as I was for the scene, not a moment was lost. In a trice, my jacket and waistcoat were off, my trousers were down at my heels, and my shirt tucked up round my waist like George's, presenting, I flattered myself, as favourable a proof of my manly prowess as he had done. Taking up the rod, he applied a few stripes to my naked posteriors, while we watched the proceedings of the girls.

Finding their escape by the principal door barred by the flaming falchion which George brandished in their faces, they made an attempt to escape by the side door. This also had been guarded against. Ascertaining that it was locked, and now catching a glimpse of the new formidable weapon, which I disclosed to their sight, and which George took care should be presented in full view, they retreated to the sofa, covered their faces with their hands, and kneeling down, ensconced themselves in each corner, burying their heads in the cushions.

In this position, though they secured the main approach to the principal scene of pleasure which they probably supposed would be the first object of attack, they forgot that the back entrance was left quite open to assault. Nor were we now at all disposed to give them quarter. While George threw himself upon Maria, I made an attack upon Eliza.

Before they were aware what we were about their petticoats were turned up and their lovely bottoms exposed to our delighted gaze. Although we did not profane them with the rod, a few slaps with our hands upon the polished ivory surfaces made them glow with a beauteous rosy tint. Ashamed of this exposure, they struggled to replace their petticoats. Nor was I at all unwilling to change the mode of attack. Throwing one arm round Eliza's waist to keep her down, and pressing my lips against her cheek, I inserted my hand beneath her petticoats as she attempted to pull them down, and gliding it up between her legs, I brought it by one rapid and decisive sweep fairly between her thighs to the very entrance, and even insinuated one finger within the lips, of the centre of attraction, before she was in the least aware of the change in my tactics.

She struggled at first, and endeavoured to rise up and get away from me. But I had secured my advantage too well to be easily defeated, and after a few unavailing attempts she gave up the contest, and seemed to resign herself to her fate.

I was not slow to avail myself of the advantage I had thus gained and, after kissing away a few tears, I contrived to insert the hand, with which I did not now find it necessary to hold her down, within the front of her gown, and proceeded to handle and toy with a most lovely pair of little, smooth, firm, bubbies, which seemed to grow harder under my burning touches.

All this time I continued to move my finger up and down in the most lascivious manner within the narrow entrance of the charming grotto into which I had managed to insert it, and the double action soon began to produce an evident effect upon her. The tears ceased to flow, and my ardent kisses, if not returned, were at least received with tokens of approbation and pleasure. Presently I felt the lips of her delicious recess contract and close upon my lascivious finger, and after a little apparent hesitation the buttocks began to move gently backwards and forwards in unison with the stimulating motions of the provoking intruder. Encouraged by this and feeling convinced that her voluptuous sensations were now carrying her onward in the path of pleasure in spite of herself, I took hold of her hand and placed it upon my burning weapon. At first she attempted to withdraw it, but I held it firmly upon the throbbing and palpitating object; and after a little struggle I prevailed upon her not only to grasp it, but also to humour the wanton movements which I made with it backwards and forwards within the grasp of her soft fingers. This delightful amusement occupied us for some little time, and I was in no hurry to bring it to a close, for I found Eliza was every moment getting more and more excited, and her actions becoming freer and less embarrassed. But I felt that if I continued it longer we must both inevitably bring on the final crisis. Having already succeeded so well in my undertaking, I was anxious that she should enjoy the supreme happiness in the most complete manner possible, and I had little doubt that her excited passions would now induce her to give every facility to my proceedings. Changing her position a little to favor my object, I abandoned the advantage I enjoyed in the rear for the purpose of obtaining a more convenient lodgement in front. Inserting one knee under her thigh, I turned her over on her back, and throwing myself upon her to prevent her from rising, though to tell the truth, she did not appear to dislike the change of posture, I again tickled her up with my finger for a minute or two. Then withdrawing it from the delicious cavity and pressing her closely to my bosom and stifling her remonstrances with kisses and caresses, I endeavored to replace the fortunate finger with the more appropriate organ, which was now fierce with desire, and burning to attain its proper position and deposit its luscious treasures within the delicious receptacle. The head was already at the entrance, and I was just flattering myself that another push or two would attain my object and complete our mutual happiness, when a confounded bell rang out loudly.

I at once foreboded that it sounded the knell of all my hopes, for that opportunity at least, nor was I far wrong. However, I took no notice of it, but continued my efforts to effect the much desired penetration. But starting up with a strength and energy she had not previously exhibited, Eliza exclaimed, "Oh, Sir Francis, you must let me go! It is the visitor's bell, and we shall be wanted immediately."

I was extremely loth to lose the opportunity, and at first was disposed to try to retain the advantage I had already gained until I had secured the victory. But the evident distress she displayed affected me. I could not help feeling from the sudden change in her manner that it was urgent necessity, and not want of inclination, that forced her to put a stop to our proceedings. When she exclaimed, "Oh, do have mercy on us! Think what would be the consequence if we were to be found in this state!" I could not resist the appeal, and allowing her to rise, I said that however greatly disappointed I might be at such an untoward termination to our amusements, I could not think of putting any contemplated enjoyment on my own part in competition with what might prove injurious to her, and that I should make no opposition to their leaving us at once, trusting that I should meet with the reward for my forebearance on some future more favourable occasion.

She thanked me warmly, and would doubtless have promised anything in order to get away, but I was not disposed to place much value upon any promises made in such a situation, and therefore did not attempt to extort any. She hastily began to arrange her dress, which had been not a little disarranged in the amorous struggle, and we then turned our glances towards George and Maria.

Whether it was that he had been more enterprising than I had been, or had met with less opposition, I know not, but when our attention was drawn to them we found Maria extended on her back on the sofa, with her legs spread wide out, and her petticoats above her waist, and George, with his trousers down about his heels and his plump white posteriors exposed to view quite bare, extended on the top of her, his legs between hers, clasping her tightly round the waist, and planting fiery kisses upon her lips, which were returned with interest. His buttocks were moving up and down with fierce heaves, and he endeavoured to effect his object and obtain admission to the virgin fortress.

At first I thought he had been more successful than I had been, but on a closer inspection, I found he was still beating about the bush, and that his weapon was still wandering in wild and hurried movements around the entrance without having yet hit upon the right spot, or managed to get within the secluded avenue of pleasure. Eliza spoke to them without producing any effect, and I was obliged to lay my hand on George's shoulder, and make him listen while I explained to him the state of matters. His answer was "Oh goodness, I can't stop now, I must get it in."

At this moment another bell rang, which Eliza told me was a signal they were wanted. There was now no help for it. I was forced to remind George that we should not only ruin the girls, but also lose all chance of having any future enjoyment with them if we allowed ourselves to be surprised on this occasion. It was with difficulty I could persuade him to get up and permit Maria to rise. He wished to keep the girls until they promised to come back to us; but as the thing must be done, I thought the sooner the better, and I therefore opened the side door and enabled them to escape to their own room where they hastened to repair the disorder in their hair and dress, which might have led to suspicion. Fortunately they were able to accomplish this and to make their appearance in the drawing room without their absence having attracted attention.

George had managed to extort a promise from Maria that they would return when the visitors departed; but not putting much faith in this, we dressed ourselves and proceeded to join them, hoping that we might be able to induce them to give us another opportunity when they were left alone. In this, however, we were disappointed. Being obliged to attend some ladies to their carriage, we found on our return that the birds had flown, nor did they make their appearance again till dinner time.

We were greatly annoyed at this unfortunate issue of our first attempt, just when it was on the very point of complete success; more especially, as every effort we could make to persuade them to give us another opportunity to accomplish our object was unavailing. It is true that all restraint among us was now removed. They laughed and joked with us, and did not take amiss the minor liberties we sometimes contrived to take with their persons. Nay, they even seemed to enjoy the fun, when occasionally, on a safe opportunity, we would produce our inflamed weapons and exhibit them in the imposing condition which their presence never failed to produce, in order to try to tempt them and to excite them to comply with our desires. Occasionally they would even allow us to place their hands upon them and make them toy and play with them; but still they took good care never to accompany us alone to any place where our efforts might be successfully renewed to accomplish the great object of our wishes.

One very hot day we took our books to enjoy the fresh air under the shade of a tree on the lawn in the front of the Abbey. We were quite near enough the house to be visible from the window, and the place was so exposed that it was out of the question to think of attempting the full gratification of our desires.

Nevertheless, we were so far off that our proceedings could not be distinctly observed, and there were a few low shrubs around which entirely concealed the lower parts of our persons, but still not so high as to prevent us from easily discovering if anyone approached us.

There was thus a fair opportunity afforded us for indulging in minor species of amusement for which we might feel inclined. Our desires, kept constantly on the stretch as they had been, were too potent to permit us to let such an opportunity escape us. George's trousers were soon unbuttoned, and his beautiful article, starting out in all its glory, was placed in Maria's hand.

After a little pretended hesitation and bashfulness, she began to get excited and interested in the lovely object, twisting her fingers among the scanty curls which adorned its root and toying with the little balls puckered up beneath, all which were freely exposed to her inspection.

For my part, I had laid my head on Eliza's lap and, slipping my hand under her petticoats, had insinuated a finger within her delicious aperture, playing with it, and tickling it, in the most wanton manner I could devise. The effects of both these operations were soon quite apparent on the lovely girls. Their eyes sparkled, and their faces became flushed, and I had very little doubt that could it have been safely done, they would have consented to gratify our fondest desires. I knew that some visitors were expected to spend the afternoon with us, who would occupy the girls and prevent any chance of further amusement for that day at least; and it occurred to me that though it would be too rash to attempt the perfect consummation of our happiness, we might at least indulge ourselves by carrying our gratification as far as we could safely venture to do so, and at all events thoroughly enjoy all the minor pleasures which were within our power. I therefore made a sign to George, which he at once understood. Following my example and getting his finger within Maria's centre of pleasure, he operated upon it in such an agreeable manner that she became excited beyond measure. Stretching herself beside him, she convulsively grasped the ivory pillar which she held in her hand, hugging and squeezing it and indulging in every variety of tender pressure. George instantly took advantage of her excitement, and while he continued to move his finger rapidly in and out of her lovely grotto, he agitated his own body so as to make his throbbing member slip backwards and forwards in the fond grasp which she maintained upon it. His involuntary exclamations of rapture and delight appeared to touch and affect Maria, and seeing how much pleasure she was giving him, as well as receiving herself, she could not refrain from trying to do everything in her power to increase his enjoyment. A word or two from him, every now and then, regulated the rapidity of their movements, and I soon saw that they were on the high road to attain that degree of bliss to which alone we could aspire under present circumstances.

Finding them so well employed, I hastened to follow their example. Unloosening my trousers, I set at liberty my champion, which was burning with impatience to join in the sport. Taking Eliza's hand, I placed it upon the throbbing object. She started with surprise and pleasure, on feeling its hot inflamed state, but did not attempt to remove her hand from where I placed it. She was sitting on the ground, with her back leaning against a tree. I gently raised up her petticoats and, slipping my hand beneath them, separated her thighs, and pressed my lips upon her springy mount and kissed it fondly. Searching out with my finger the most sensitive part, I played with it and tickled it until it swelled out and became inflamed to the utmost degree.

I soon ascertained the successful effect of my operations by the delightful manner in which she rewarded me, compressing my organ of manhood in her charming grasp in the most delicious manner possible and meeting and humouring the hurried and frantic thrusts with which I made it move to and fro between her fingers.

Finding that she was quite willing to continue the operations, which afforded us both so much enjoyment, I raised myself up on my knees, and while I gazed in her lovely countenance, sparkling with all the fires of luxurious delight, I exhibited to her the full proportions of my foaming champion as it bounded up and down under the fierce excitement of the delicious pressure she exercised upon it. I had intended to have made her witness the final outburst of the tide of pleasure. And, therefore, while I kept up the pleasing irritation with my finger, I purposely delayed bringing on with her the final crisis. But as I felt the flood of rapture ready to pour from me, I could restrain myself no longer, and hastily drawing up her petticoats before she could make any opposition, I bent forward and threw myself down across her. My stiff and bursting instrument penetrated between her thighs, and deposited its boiling treasure at the very mouth of the abode of bliss. As the stream of pleasure continued to flow out from me in successive jets, I felt Eliza's body give a gentle shiver under me. We lay wrapt in bliss for some minutes, during which she made no attempt to dislodge me from my situation. I guessed what had happened to her; but to make certain, I again placed my finger within her aperture and found the interior quite moist with a liquid which I knew had not issued from me.

When I put the question to her, she acknowledged with burning blushes that from the excited state she had been in, the touch of my burning weapon so near the critical spot had applied the torch to the fuel ready to burst into flame, and had brought on with her the final bliss at the very same time with me.

As I wiped away the dewy effusion from her thighs, I tenderly reproached her with having allowed it to be wasted in such an unsatisfactory manner, when it might have afforded so much greater gratification to us both. I could read in the pleased and yet longing expression of her lovely eyes that such a consummation would have been no less agreeable to her than to me; and I could fancy that were a favourable opportunity to offer itself, there would now be no great objection on her part to allow the wondrous instrument of pleasure, on which she again gazed with surprise and admiration as it throbbed and beat in her fond grasp, to take the necessary measures to procure for us both the highest gratification of which human nature is susceptible.

On casting my eyes around to where George and Maria were placed, I saw that we were still in time to enjoy a delightful spectacle to which I hastened to call the attention of my companion. George was stretched at full length on his back on the ground. The front of his trousers was quite open, disclosing all the lower part of his belly and his thighs. His charming weapon protruded stiff and erect up from the few short curls which had begun to adorn it. Maria was kneeling astride of him, grasping in her hand the instrument of bliss, and urging her fingers up and down upon it with an impetuosity that betokened the fierce fire that was raging within her. George's operations upon her we could not discern, for his head was buried between her thighs, and was entirely concealed by her petticoats, which fell over it. But that he was employed on a similar operation was quite evident from the short hurried movements which her posteriors kept up, no doubt in response to the luxurious and provoking touches of his penetrating finger. Maria's face was bent down within a few inches of the object of her adoration, upon which she was too intent to take any notice of us.

We enjoyed for a minute or two the pleasing contemplation of her delightful occupation and of the libidinous heaves of George's buttocks, which increased in strength and rapidity as the critical moment began with him. At length it arrived, and accompanied with an exclamation of rapture, the creamy jet issued forth from him with an energy that made it fly up, and bedew the countenance of the astonished Maria. Retaining her grasp, she gazed for an instant with rapture on this unexpected phenomenon; but her time was come too, and almost before George's tide had ceased to flow, she sank down upon him, pressing his still stiff and erect weapon to her lips, and showering kisses upon it while, as we soon found, she repaid George's exertions with a tender effusion from her own private resources, which somewhat calmed her senses and restored her to reason.

When we had a little recovered ourselves, the girls appeared to be rather ashamed of the excesses which they had committed. And as George continued to tease them not a little, regarding the sacrilege they had been guilty of in thus wastefully pouring out both their own and our treasures, they soon took refuge in the house to hide their blushes and confusion.

We soon found, however, that though still too frightened to allow us to proceed to the last extremity, they would have no objection to a renewal of our late exploit. But this did not suit the purpose of George and myself, and we were determined not to allow them thus to tantalize us and slip through our fingers, now that we had obtained such a hold over them.

After some days' fruitless endeavours to effect our object, we became aware that we must again resort to stratagem for success. But the difficulty was how to accomplish it, for after having been once entrapped, they were now upon their guard with us.

We had taken down with us some of the best amatory pictures we could procure, and on the night of the flogging scene, when we found we could not prevail on them to return with us to the library, George had told them that we were not going to imitate their cruelty but would do all in our power to amuse them, and that he would accordingly deposit the pictures in the old hiding place that they might inspect them whenever they felt disposed. We kept a watch upon them, but without any great hope of immediate success from the stratagem, as we were aware they would suspect us and would take care not to be caught looking at them. We soon discovered however, from the marks we placed, that they were in the habit of amusing themselves with those pictures when they were certain we were out of the way, and we laid our plans accordingly.

One morning it was announced at breakfast time that the old ladies were going to dine that day at the house of a friend some miles off, so that the young people would be left quite alone for the whole evening. Although we were perfectly aware of this, and had founded our scheme upon it, we affected not to have known it. George turning to me said, "Oh Frank, this will suit us nicely. Mrs. Montague will perhaps be good enough to allow us to dine at luncheon time, and by that hour the river will be in prime fishing order after the rain, and we shall have a good afternoon's sport." Mrs. Montague at once agreed and gave orders accordingly. I thought the young ladies looked rather blank at this announcement, and I told George to whisper to Maria that if they would promise to be kind to us, we would return at seven o'clock to take tea with them when we would have the house all to ourselves. This satisfied them and put them off their guard.

All proceeded as we hoped. After luncheon we started for the river, and plied our rods as effectually as we could, in order that we might have something to show on our return. When the time approached at which the old ladies were to leave the Abbey, we returned to it; and hiding our fishing apparatus in one of the plantations, we made our way into the library by the window which we had purposely left open. We then concealed ourselves in a large closet of which there were two, one on each side of the window. We knew we could accomplish this without discovery as the girls would then be engaged assisting the old ladies to dress.

Having safely ensconced ourselves in our hiding place, we waited patiently at first for the departure of the old people. In a short time the carriage came to the door, and soon after we heard it drive off. We now became very impatient, for we confidently trusted that the girls would take advantage of such a favourable opportunity of being left entirely to themselves to derive some amusement from an inspection of the pictures, to which George had told them the night before that he had added some new ones, and we had taken care they should have no opportunity of looking at them that day. Imagine therefore our dismay when we heard them leave their own room, proceed to the front door, and issue forth, closing it after them somewhat loudly.

George was in a sad state of vexation, and proposed that we should follow them, but this I objected to, saying that we should have plenty of time if we were obliged to go to work openly, and it was well worth while to wait patiently for some time longer for the chance of taking them at such advantage as would place them entirely in our power. George acquiesced and agreed to remain quiet. But his patience had nearly forsaken him when we heard the side door, which gave access to the library from the garden, gently open. We were in a state of anxious suspense until we heard it close, and beheld Maria's face peep through the door of the library. Finding all apparently safe, she came into the room and was immediately followed by Eliza. They closed the door softly, and we at once anticipated complete success as soon as we saw them draw the bolts of both it and the principal door. Our impatience was now extreme, but seeing everything proceeding so favourably, we resolved to curb it until we were in a situation to make the most of the advantage we had calculated on gaining. We therefore remained perfectly quiet, watching their proceedings.

Apparently satisfied that there was no occasion for any restraint upon their actions, they threw off all disguise and, removing their bonnets, proceeded to open the secret place and take out the pictures. They inspected them for some minutes, evidently with great pleasure, and the luscious details of the libidinous scenes they saw there depicted soon produced their natural effect upon them. After some little preliminaries, Maria laid herself back at full length upon the sofa, stretching out her legs before her, and drew up her petticoats as far as they would go; and at the same time pulled up the petticoats of Eliza, who was sitting beside her turning over the pictures, in such a manner to exhibit her thighs, belly, and the beautiful cleft with its surrounding fringe of curly hair. She inserted a finger into it and proceeded to titillate it, while with her other hand, she operated a similar diversion on her own charming aperture.

This was too much for us to view, and stand longer inactive. We had quite divested ourselves of the whole of our clothes, and softly opening the door, we rushed out perfectly naked, and with splendidly erected weapons threw ourselves at once upon our defenceless prey. They were so utterly taken by surprise, and so confounded at the state in which we appeared before them and the situation in which they themselves had been discovered, that they were perfectly unable to stir, and remained motionless in the same attitudes until we had clasped them in our arms and pressed them to our breasts, without their having the power to make the slightest resistance.

Maria's position, stretched at full length on the sofa, with her legs hanging down and wide apart, was too tempting to be resisted. In an instant George was between her thighs, his arms clasped around her waist, his naked belly rubbing against hers, and his fiery champion pressed against the lower part of her belly, endeavouring to find an entrance to that abode of bliss from which he had just snatched her finger, with the intention to replace it with a more satisfactory and appropriate organ.

For my part, though equally desirous to profit by the occasion, I was still cool enough to decide upon the best course of procedure. There was only one sofa in the room, so that only one pair could, with comfort and satisfaction, proceed with the pleasing operation. George was so maddened with excitement that I saw he could brook no delay, and I resolved that I should allow him to accomplish without hindrance his first victory in the field of Venus. I was the more induced to do this from the consideration that the exploration my finger had already made on the former occasions had convinced me that the fortress I had to attack was to be approached by an entrance so straight and narrow that the passage of my battering ram into the breach was not likely to be effected without considerable difficulty, and some suffering on the part of the besieged party. From George's account, there was not likely to be the same difficulty with regard to Maria, partly because her entrance was more open and partly because his member had not yet attained the same size as mine.

All these considerations made me think it advisable to secure every advantage by having Eliza favourably placed in a convenient position on the sofa before I attempted the assault; and I thought likewise that the previous sight of the raptures, which I was certain George and Maria would experience and exhibit before her, would encourage her and reconcile her to any little suffering she might undergo in becoming qualified to enjoy a similar bliss. I therefore sat down on the sofa, and keeping her petticoats still raised up, I made Eliza sit down, with her naked bottom on my knees, and slipped my instrument between her thighs so as to make it rub against the lips of her lovely aperture. At the same time I whispered to her that I thought we had better allow George and Maria to enjoy themselves in the first place, as there was not room for us all on the sofa at the same time.

She was in such a state of confusion and distraction, arising from the shame at having been detected in her previous occupation, as well as from the exciting nature of the novel scene now presented before her eyes of two handsome youths exhibiting all their naked charms, that she was in no condition to resist anything I required. But wishing to keep up her excitement to the utmost, I now directed her attention to the proceedings of our companions.

Maria apparently now thought that it was no use to mince matters, and that as the operation must be gone through, she might as well enjoy it thoroughly. Accordingly, instead of making any resistance, she had clasped her arms round George's naked body, and with burning kisses was animating him to his task, while the forward movements of her buttocks to meet his thrusts, showed that her anxiety was fully equal to his that they should effect an immediate and pleasing conjunction. I saw, however, that in their inexperience they were still beating about the bush, and had not yet taken the proper means to introduce the impatient stallion into the opening that was thus left quite free for his reception. I said to George, "Wait a minute, my boy, I think I could manage to place you in a more satisfactory position."

Throwing my arms round the legs of both, I lifted them up and placed them in an advantageous position on the sofa. Then inserting my hand between their bellies, I laid hold of George's fiery weapon, and keeping it directed right upon the proper spot, I told him to thrust away now. This he did with hearty good will. The first thrust he was within the lips, the second he was half way in, and the third he was so fairly engulphed, that I had to let go my hold, and withdraw my hand, so as to admit of their perfect conjunction.

At the first thrust Maria met him with a bound of her buttocks, at the second she uttered a scream, and as he penetrated her interior at the third, she beseeched him to stop, saying that he was killing her. George, however, was not now in a state to be able to listen to her remonstrances. Satisfied that the worst was over and his object fully gained, as much to her benefit as his own, he merely replied with repeated fierce heaves and thrusts, while his fiery kisses seemed intended to stifle her complaints. A very few movements of his weapon, driven in as it was from point to hilt within her, were sufficient to drown all sense of suffering, and to rekindle the flame of desire which had previously animated her. Very soon her impetuous and lascivious motions rivalled his own in force and activity, as straining each other in their close embrace they strove to drive the newly-inserted wedge still further and further into the abode of bliss. Maria's upward heaves and the impetuous motions of George's bounding buttocks, as they kept time together at each luscious thrust, soon produced their pleasing effect, and with a cry of rapture, the enamored boy, drowned in a sea of delight, poured forth his blissful treasures, while the no less enchanted girl, wrought up to an equal pitch of boundless pleasure, responded to his maiden tribute by shedding forth the first effusion ever drawn from her by manly vigour, a happy consummation which was accompanied on both sides with the most lively demonstrations of perfect delight.

While they were thus so agreeably occupied, I had been almost as much so in watching the effect which this luxurious scene produced upon Eliza, and in doing all in my power, by directing her attention to the various symptoms of enjoyment they exhibited and by caressing and toying with her in the most luxurious manner I could devise, in order to prepare her fully for following out the good example set before us. I had determined, if possible, to add to my pleasure by reducing her to the same state of nature in which I was myself. At first she objected to my removing her clothes. But soon getting excited with observing the wanton proceedings of George and Maria, as was clearly evinced to me by the tender squeezes she gave to my sensitive plant, which I insisted on her holding in her hand, she ceased to make any opposition to my proceedings. I therefore managed to remove her stays, and to unloosen all the fastenings of her dress, so that her petticoats hung loosely about her.

While George and Maria lay motionless in the blissful trance which follows the thorough completion of our fondest desires, I made Eliza rise from my knee, on which her petticoats slipped down, leaving her nothing but her chemise as a covering. This I also attempted to remove, but she insisted on being allowed to retain this last protection to her maiden modesty.

George, immediately on recovering his senses, started up and, disengaging himself from Maria, exhibited to us his conquering weapon, still erect and covered with semen slightly tinged with the gory marks of his triumphant success. On seeing the state of matters, and divining my object, he exclaimed, "Oh, this will be capital; it will be such fun to see you two at it naked."

Coming to my assistance, he occupied Eliza's attention by threatening an attack upon her still virgin citadel, under cover of which I had no difficulty in slipping her chemise over her head.

Intent upon now accomplishing the desired object, I clasped her naked form in my arms, and pressed my glowing body against hers with all the ardour of youthful desire. George assisted Maria to rise from the sofa, which was no sooner left vacant than I laid my not unwilling partner upon it, and separating her thighs, got between them and applied love's arrow to the appropriate mark.

Seeing that I was on the point of commencing operations, George said to Maria, "Come, let us try if we can't give him a little of the kind assistance he rendered us. I shall keep the lips open while you shall hold the rudder in its proper place."

Presently I felt the mouth of the opening distended, making way for the point of my weapon to press forward, while Maria's left hand pressed the shaft and tickled the depending balls. I then heard Maria say, "What is the reason, George, that yours is not so big as this?"

"Never do you mind!" was his reply; "it is quite big enough for you, as you found not long ago, and it will be as big as his when I am as old as he is."

"You are quite right, my dear fellow," said I. "I don't think mine was as big as yours is now when I was your age. And it was just as well for Maria that it is not bigger, as it has saved her some of the pain which I am afraid I must inflict upon my little darling here, before we can enjoy the same pleasure you have done; but I am sure she will believe me when I tell her that I shall spare her as much as I possibly can, and that it will be nothing compared with the pleasure she will enjoy when we are once fairly united."

"Oh, I shan't pity her at all!" said Maria. "I am sure I would suffer ten times as much as I did, most willingly, for the same pleasure."

I was meanwhile proceeding with the operation as satisfactorily as I could expect. George and Maria performed their parts capitally and kept everything in due order, so that I had merely to press forward, which I did as rapidly as I could venture upon in the circumstances. I found the entrance as narrow and as difficult to force as I had anticipated, but the obstructions gradually gave way before the steady pressure forwards which I applied, until I had reached nearly half way in. Then I was forced to come to a stop for a moment, while I endeavoured to pacify her struggles and soothe her anguish, by assuring her that it would soon be over, and she would be made perfectly happy. I felt, however, that a vigorous effort must still be made to achieve the final victory; and the swollen and almost bursting state of my virile member gave me warning that unless this effort was speedily made, the opportunity might be lost for the present at least.

Satisfied that it was better for my companion to have the worst over at once, I kissed her fondly, and straining her to my body with all my power, I pushed forward with a steady pressure, driving on my fiery steed with all the impetus I could give him, till he fairly burst the opposing barriers and forced his triumphant way into her inmost recesses.

I had no sooner done so than the warm flesh of the virgin recess closing around the entire circumference of my intruding member in the most delicious manner, forced the tide of joy to burst from me. I sank upon her bosom in the height of bliss, while the poor suffering girl, entirely overcome with the pain of the sudden smart occasioned by the opening up of this narrow passage, after giving vent to a shriek wrung from her by the intense suffering, closed her eyes and lay motionless under me, as if she had fainted.

When the first overpowering sensations of intense bliss had subsided a little, I endeavoured to recall the swooning girl to her senses, and the first sharp pang of agony having passed away, she soon showed symptoms of recovery. Thinking that the only way to recompense her for her suffering, was to make her, as speedily as possible, partake in the raptures she had afforded me, I ventured to move gently once or twice backwards and forwards within her; the first time I did so, she winced again and with difficulty suppressed a scream; but after two or three repetitions performed in a slow and gentle manner, she acknowledged that the intruder no longer hurt her.

Encouraged by this, I was proceeding more vigorously; when George, seeing that I was fully intent on running a second course, exclaimed, "Come, come, this is not fair; it is our turn now."

"No, no, my dear boy," replied I, "you had the first opportunity, and it is only fair that we should begin first this time; besides Eliza has had no enjoyment yet, and I am afraid that after what she has suffered, she will never allow me to get in again, if I let her off without making her fully sensible of all the pleasure her new acquaintance can give her now that he is fairly lodged in the proper quarter."

"Well, well," replied he, "go on, only make haste, for Maria is tickling me up at such a rate that I am afraid she will make me part with my treasure too soon, without being able to give her the benefit of it."

I did not require any further stimulus to urge me on in the path of pleasure. The whole lascivious scene we had gone through, and the tight pressure which the virgin sheath exerted upon my burning priapus, excited my lustful propensities to the utmost, so that even my recent effusion had hardly perceptibly diminished my vigorous powers. Gradually increasing the force and velocity of my thrusts, I worked away up and down in the narrow receptacle, which, now lubricated by my plentiful emission, afforded an easier passage for the delighted member which was procuring us so much pleasure. I had very soon the satisfaction of finding that his operations were not only harmless, but that they even seemed to afford delight to my darling girl. By degrees, her embrace round me was tightened, her lips returned my luxurious pressures, her buttocks began to heave in unison with mine; at first keeping pace with my movements, but soon agitating themselves up and down in a still more rapid and lascivious manner.

Observing these symptoms of the approach of pleasure, I redoubled my efforts and quickened my motions, so as to accelerate the progress of the internal operation, and just as I felt the second tide of rapture bursting from me, she uttered a cry—not this time the signal of pain, but of the most extreme delight; and after a prolonged upward heave, as if she wished to ram still more of the pleasure giver within her, she sank back on the sofa in the utmost extasy, enjoying to the fullest extent the blissful delight of the first complete sexual enjoyment she had ever tasted.

She remained so long in the agony of pleasure that I was able gradually to withdraw the instrument of her martyrdom and of her delight, and to wipe away the mingled stream of blood and semen which followed its removal, before she was conscious of my proceedings.

It was fortunate that the scene of operations was covered with crimson leather, so that no stain was left upon it, or we should probably have got into a sad scrape.

George and Maria were too intent upon a renewal of their amusement, to allow her any longer repose. Seeing their impatience to begin again, I hastily raised Eliza in my arms and, placing her upon my knee, sat down to witness the repetition of the deed they had already performed. Taking a hint from our proceedings, George had by this time stripped Maria entirely naked. On this occasion they required no assistance in the operation. Maria herself guided George's weapon to the mark, and he no sooner found the lips parting, than bending forward with extatic delight, he penetrated her interior with one thrust, and never ceased his exertions till their mutual exclamations of satisfaction and delight showed that this encounter had not fallen short of the last in point of rapture and bliss.

While they ran their second amorous course, Eliza's curious hand was easily induced to occupy itself with caressing the strange machine which had just afforded her so much pleasure. A few touches and wanton pressures sufficed to make it regain its former state of vigour and erection. Although at first she declared she was afraid to permit it again to enter within her now no longer virgin recess, she was soon persuaded to allow me to make the attempt, and by a little management and address I contrived to satisfy her that it could now make its way within and renew all her pleasurable sensations without any risk of a repetition of the so much dreaded first painful impressions. Protruding up between her thighs, and its coral head nestled within the charming recess, the wicked little monster remained quiescent during the remainder of George's engagement with Maria, the exciting scene making him occasionally give a bound upwards, till he was quite engulphed. No sooner were they induced to quit the post of pleasure, than without loosening the pleasant tie which bound us together, I placed Eliza again on the sofa, and afforded her a pleasing repetition of our former enjoyment. This delighted her even more than the last; for being unaccompanied by the slightest tinge of pain, she was enabled fully to enjoy all the blissful and maddening sensations which her new acquaintance was calculated to confer upon her, while stirring up the seeds of joy in her sensitive region.

A third encounter was satisfactorily concluded by both sets of combatants with unabated delight. After this, the girls declared that they must leave us, as their longer absence would be noticed by the servants. Though unwilling to part from them, we were not much disposed to object to this, as we were both beginning to feel that a slight respite would be necessary to enable us to carry on the war with satisfactory vigour. And we still anticipated an opportunity for further amusement before the time the old ladies should arrive. We therefore allowed them to go; and after regaining our fishing apparatus, made our appearance as if just returned from the river and repaired to our rooms to change our dress.

When we entered the drawing room we found the preparations for tea all ready on the table, and the girls waiting for us. We had a good laugh at the awkward manner in which they moved across the room to the tea table, which plainly showed that our pastimes, however pleasing, had still left some remains of stiffness, which we at once declared nothing but a repetition of the same exercise would remove. As a matter of course I devoted myself to Eliza, who was busy making tea, leaving George to entertain Maria, which he proceeded to do in the most agreeable manner. My back was turned to them, and I did not observe what they were about till my attention was called to their operations by observing the colour coming and going on Eliza's cheeks, and the evident confusion she was in. Turning round, what should I find but the young rogue stretched out at full length on an easy chair, with his legs extended before him, and his trousers down at his heels, while Maria, with her petticoats tucked up round her waist, was seated astride him, impaled upon the pleasant stake with which she had recently renewed her acquaintance and which, stiff and erect as ever, again penetrated her vitals.

I at once exclaimed against this proceeding as running such a risk of discovery, but I found the young libertine was more prudent than I gave him credit for; and had already ascertained from Maria that he was quite safe. It appeared that there was a party at one of the farmer's houses that evening, and some of the female servants had applied to their young mistresses for leave to go to it.

The girls saw clearly the advantage to be gained by having the coast clear for that evening, and willingly gave the desired permission, not only to those who applied for it, but also to the one who should have waited on us at tea, promising that they themselves would remove the tea things to the butler's pantry, the menservants having gone with their mistress. They only stipulated that they should return in time not to be missed.

Finding the opportunity so favourable, I lost no time in following the agreeable example they had set us, taking the precaution first to lock the door. Drawing another easy chair to the table, I stretched myself out on it in a similar manner, and pulled down my trousers till my manly weapon stood out along my belly uncovered and firm and erect. I then raised up Eliza's petticoats, and made her take up her position across me with a leg on each side. After a few caresses on both sides, taking hold of my weapon, I held it straight upright, at right angles to my belly, and applying it to the mark, made Eliza sink down gradually upon it, and make herself fast to me by the most charming bond, the key fitting into the lock in the most delicious manner possible.

When this was fairly accomplished, I allowed her to remain quiet in this position, and proceed with her tea making operations. We all found this an extremely agreeable arrangement; but before our first cup of tea was finished, it became very evident that sundry shoves and heaves which were given on both sides sadly interfered with the work of carrying the cup to the lips, and rendered it necessary that a certain operation of a different kind should be performed between another pair of lips, before the fair riders and their unruly steeds could satisfactorily indulge their tea drinking propensities.

A regular race then ensued to ascertain which of the two couples should first reach the goal of pleasure, in which the fair jockies exerted themselves with the utmost animation, and which ended in a dead heat.

The fire of the coursers having been somewhat tamed by this proceeding, they were allowed to remain quiet in their most agreeable stables until tea was concluded. By this time having again become mutinous, and lifting up their proud heads as if challenging another contest, their fair riders were no ways disinclined to afford them a further opportunity of distinguishing themselves in the course of pleasure. There was no occasion for whipping and spurring. Gently rising in the saddle, and then again sinking down, so as always to preserve their firm hold over their bounding steeds, they roused them up to the highest pitch of excitement and were amply rewarded for the pleasure they gave by the corresponding efforts which their animated proceedings drew from their generous steeds. I believe the contest ended by Eliza bringing in her dripping courser a short space in advance of her competitor; but all parties were so much overpowered by the delicious enjoyment which was the result of the struggle that they were hardly conscious of what was happening to one another.

Readjusting our clothes, and getting quit of the tea things, we then sat down for a short time to the piano, when a few songs of the warmest and most impassioned nature again set us agog, and necessitated another application of the cooling liniment to the wanton spot of pleasure. Our amorous pranks were, however, now put a stop to by the return of the old ladies. Warned by the sound of the carriage wheels on the gravel, we adjusted ourselves in proper positions and were found by them performing a very different sort of duet from that which had occupied the two couples all the previous part of the evening.

When the ladies arrived, we learnt, to our dismay, that the house was to be filled with company the following day.

They had met with some friends, whose visit in the neighbourhood had been cut short by the dangerous illness of the lady in whose house they were residing, and it had been hastily arranged that the whole party should, in the meantime, take up their abode in the Abbey.

This greatly annoyed us; for all restraint being now banished from among us, we had calculated upon many a happy hour being spent in the library, which was hardly ever visited by the old ladies; and we sadly feared that the presence of so many visitors would prove a great hindrance —if it did not put a complete stop—to our pleasant intercourse.

But matters turned out more favourably than we anticipated and the very event we dreaded only tended to increase our happiness. At breakfast the next morning there was some discussion as to where the different visitors were to be accommodated, a difficulty arising in consequence of two of them requiring rooms on the ground floor, both being unable to mount upstairs with ease, the one from fat and the other from lameness. As our rooms were on that floor, we thought ourselves constrained to offer to vacate them; but fortunately they were not considered eligible, being thought more suitable for gentlemen than ladies, from their being detached from the other sleeping apartments. The matter was arranged by the fat lady getting an unoccupied room and the lame one and her niece getting two adjoining apartments, which had hitherto been occupied by Miss Vivian and the young ladies. Miss Vivian took another apartment upstairs, and the girls were to occupy a room above the library, which had formerly been used as their nursery.

I had been somewhat struck with the peculiar construction of the building, of which I had taken some sketches, and had especially noticed one peculiarity—that all the rooms had two accesses, opening either into the passages or into the adjoining room.

On finding that the girls were to be separated from Miss Vivian, it occurred to me that it would be desirable to ascertain whether this peculiarity might not be turned to account so as to enable us to get access to our loves during the night, when alone we could hope to enjoy our mutual bliss in peace and safety. I therefore made them point out to me where their new habitation was to be; and on observing its locality, my hopes were greatly raised by what I discovered.

The main building of the house consisted of three sides of a square, along the interior of which ran a gallery on each floor looking inwards, so that all the rooms looked outwards. The library was in a sort of tower, at one angle, which was a story higher than the rest of the building. There was a large unoccupied room above the library, and above that again were situated the nursery, as it was called, and another room. The principal entrance to those rooms above the library had been closed up, and the only access at present to the nursery was by a winding staircase in a sort of turret at one corner of the tower. Our apartments were in a detached addition on the other side of the tower from this staircase, and at the angle which adjoined my room there was a similar turret, to which a door in my room appeared to open, but which was kept locked. I was in hopes there might be another staircase communicating with this door, and leading to the upper apartments.

I mentioned my idea to George, who was delighted with the prospect it held out. I told him that it would be very desirable if we could pay a visit to the girls' room, so as to discover exactly how matters stood and ascertain if there really was any communication by the turret adjoining my room. He said he could easily accomplish this, as I had not yet visited the haunted room, and he would apply for the key that he might show it to me.

The haunted room was the one immediately above the library. It was a large apartment, and at one time had been used as a sort of banqueting room, but had long been abandoned and shut up in consequence of a neighbouring proprietor having been killed in a drunken brawl, whose ghost was said still to haunt the room.

George contrived to arrange that the girls should accompany us in our exploration. We first proceeded to their room, and to our great delight, I was confirmed in my belief, by finding that the upper story consisted of two rooms, apparently similar to each other, and having a door of communication, which, however, was locked. To my questions, the girls replied that in the other room there was also a door similar to the one which communicated with the turret in their room, and I had no doubt this door led to another staircase in the corresponding turret. I therefore determined to make the attempt at least to find our way from my room to theirs by this means.

Finding ourselves alone with the girls, we endeavoured to persuade them to allow us to satisfy the natural desires which their presence occasioned; but though they were strongly tempted by the potent arguments we produced to enforce our request, they were too much alarmed at the risk of being discovered with us in their room to allow us to proceed to extremities.

Respecting their fears, we desisted from our entreaties, and then descended to the haunted chamber, which must at one time have been a handsome room, but from which the furniture had been removed with the exception of some old tapestry and a few paintings on the panels. After examining these, we again fell to work caressing the girls when George said there could be no fear of being surprised there, as none of the servants dared enter that room and the old ladies were too much occupied with making the necessary arrangements for their guests to think of coming there. The girls admitted that this was the case, but stated the difficulty that, as there was no furniture in the room, they would have to lie down on the floor, which would be sure to soil their dresses and lead to suspicion.

On looking round the room, I saw that the only article it contained was a large heavy stand for flowers, which, however, I thought might be made to answer our purpose. Telling George to lock the door, and take out the key, I took hold of Eliza, and made her lean her hands upon the stand, and bend forwards, so as to make her posteriors project. Then turning up her petticoats over her back, I exposed her beautiful white buttocks to the light. Kneeling down, I pressed my lips upon them, and inserting my face between her thighs, I kissed her beautiful mount, while I hastily unloosened my trousers, and tucking up my shirt, exposed my erect priapus and prepared for an assault. Regaining a standing position, I spread her thighs asunder, and taking my place between them, I introduced my weapon from behind, between her lovely buttocks and, putting my hand in front, distended the lips of her charming cleft, so as to enable me to insert the point. This was no sooner accomplished, than by a few fierce shoves, I easily satisfied her that our object could be perfectly attained in this manner, by effecting the insertion of the whole of my weapon in her delightful receptacle, until my balls knocked against her thighs and our flesh was brought into the most delightful contact. My thrusts forward were soon responded to by her impetuous heaves backwards, and the delicious wriggle of her splendid bottom roused me up to an excess of furious delight.

George and Maria lost no time in following our example, and established themselves in a similar position on the opposite side of the stand, so that we could watch each other's proceedings. The stand was hollow in the centre, with nothing to intercept the view, and while engaged in the same process it was a lovely sight to behold Maria's white belly and the upper part of her beautiful little cleft surrounded with its mossy border, with the white shaft of George's weapon appearing and disappearing through the curly fringe, as he drove it backwards and forwards into the sheath of pleasure. Our impassioned heaves and struggles soon produced their usual luxurious effect, and we had to grasp our partners tightly round the middle, to prevent them from giving way under the delicious effects of the melting stream which we poured into them, and to which they responded with the utmost delight.

Uncertain when we might have another opportunity for a similar enjoyment, we insisted on retaining our positions for a second round of pleasure, and we met with but faint opposition from our not yet satisfied companions. The delight they enjoyed was excessive on finding the introduction of their pleasing favourite no longer attended with any symptoms of discomfort, and producing a superlative degree of pleasure far beyond the utmost they had ever anticipated. They both did everything in their power to render not only their own, but also our happiness as complete as possible, and we had every reason to be satisfied with the manner in which they entered into the spirit of the sport and forwarded our exertions to produce our mutual delight. Our frantic heaves and throbs were received and returned with equally voluptuous and pleasure-conferring shoves and wriggles, which gradually increased in force and intensity, until the final crisis again overtook us, and we all melted away in the glorious excess of rapture.

Our fair friends were then obliged to leave us to attend to the preparations for the visitors, and I repaired to my own room to try whether I could not manage to open up a communication between it and their new sleeping place, which we now desired to make the scene of our future revels; but no effort I could make with anything in the shape of a turnscrew which my gun-case afforded, or anything I could convert into a picklock, had the slightest effect on the obstinate lock of the door, which I supposed led in the wished for direction.

Determined not to give up the project without making a fair trial, I mounted my horse, and proceeded to a small town a few miles from the Abbey, where I procured a stout turnscrew, a few picklocks, a little wax and oil, and a dark lantern, which I resolved to make use of as soon as I had an opportunity.

The experience of the first day was sufficient to convince us that, as we had feared, the presence of the visitors prevented us from seeing almost anything of our young friends in private, and our anxiety was redoubled to procure an opportunity for meeting them quietly during the night.

As soon as the other inmates of the house had retired to rest, I set to work with the picklocks, but my skill with the burglars' instruments proved very limited, and I could not succeed in opening the lock of the first door. Fortunately it was an old-fashioned one, merely fastened on with screw nails on the side next me; and I soon managed to extract the screws and remove the lock. To our great satisfaction we found that the door led, as we expected, to a small staircase, similar to that at the other corner of the tower. With the assistance of the dark lantern, we then ascertained that there were also doors of communication with the library and the haunted chamber, and ascending higher up, we found another door, which we had no doubt must communicate with the room adjoining that occupied by the girls. On the lock of this door we exerted our utmost efforts for upwards of an hour, without success. It resisted every attempt we made to pick it, and the lock being fastened on the inside we could not remove it. At length it occurred to me that the locks of both doors were probably similar, and returning down stairs, I took to pieces the one I had removed and examined its construction. I soon ascertained the manner in which it worked, and found that by a slight alteration in one of the picklocks I could easily open it. Returning to the other door, I practised the same movement upon it, and very soon succeeded in forcing back the bolt. To our infinite satisfaction we found ourselves in the apartment next that of the girls, and discovered under the door of communication, a sheet of white paper, which we had told them to place there if all was safe for us to proceed with our enterprise. As I was required to take off this lock at any rate, I lost no time in attempting to pick it but at once unscrewed the nails, and in a few minutes we found ourselves in the presence of our charmers, who were safely ensconced in bed and waiting in anxious suspense for the accomplishment of our labours, the partial success of which they had discovered from the noise we made in removing the last lock.

Eager as we were to rush into their arms, we were still obliged to submit to a short delay, for, owing to the passage having been long closed up, the operations we had been engaged in had covered our persons with so much dust and dirt that we should have left behind us unpleasant tokens of our presence had we ventured to touch either our fair friends or the snow-white linen in which they were enveloped. Telling them the reason which occasioned this unpleasant delay, we hastily retreated to our rooms and performed our ablutions, taking the opportunity at the same time to remove our habiliments; and we returned upstairs merely in our shirts and dressing gowns.

As soon as we reached their rooms, even these garments were laid aside, and naked as the moment we came into the world, we jumped into the large bed which contained our charmers, and strained them in our loving arms.

After a storm of kisses and caresses, which were mutually lavished on all sides, we proceeded to disencumber them from all useless coverings, in order that we might enjoy in perfection the reward of our labours.

This was very soon accomplished, and the shutters being closed carefully and the curtains drawn so as to prevent the light betraying us, we lighted some additional candles we had provided, and hastened to avail ourselves of the rights we had earned by our exertions and which were most willingly conceded to us.

We were too impatient to spend much time in admiring the beauties which were freely exposed to our gaze, but mounting on top of our respective fair ones, we at once plunged our weapons into the well-fitting scabbards and proceeded to urge on our chargers at a furious rate. The rapidity of this operation soon produced a copious discharge on all sides.

A little cooled by this, we disengaged ourselves from our sweet bonds, and devoted some time to an attentive survey of all those beauties of which we had now obtained full possession. Every portion of their bodies was passed under review, and each lovely charm drew forth our earnest commendations and was subjected to the warmest and most lascivious caresses. Nor did we, in our turn, escape from the same searching examination.

Maria's curiosity was openly displayed, and a little encouragement soon induced her, and even Eliza, to pursue their researches until they had fairly investigated and thoroughly understood the mechanism of all those secret parts, the nature of which is generally so very carefully attempted to be hid from young ladies.

We agreed that by way of heightening the pleasure we should now join in the amorous encounter by turns, and endeavour mutually to add to each other's enjoyment during the process. Eliza and I were the first to commence. I again got upon her, and fixed my weapon in the sheath. I then made Maria place herself on her knees, with her legs astride Eliza's head, so that during the whole operation my face was in close contact with her beautiful mount, while I kissed and caressed all her lovely charms. Making George kneel on the bed beside us, I placed Eliza's hand upon his rampant hero and made her play with the dependent jewels, until the agony of pleasure came upon her and drove everything else from her thoughts, forcing her to abandon even that pleasing amusement.

I was so excited with this lustful proceeding that finding my vigour still sufficient for another encounter, I could not make up my mind to quit such pleasing quarters as long as I could retain possession of them. Merely ceasing my active operations during the process of emission, I thrust away again with renewed earnestness and force, until I again brought my darling companion, as well as myself, to undergo the delightful sensations of a joint overflow.

On my withdrawing from my delicious position, George took his place on top of Maria and, transfixing her with his lance of pleasure, proceeded to follow our example. Observing that my worn-out charger bore evident marks of exhaustion from his continued exertions, and knowing that I had little time to spare that night for such pleasing enjoyments, he declared that he must try what he could do to re-animate its forces.

He therefore made me kneel down in front of him across Maria's head, in the same way as she had done over Eliza, and as he proceeded with his lascivious course of heaves in and out of the cavity of his charmer, he took the point of my weapon in his mouth. Eliza was made to kneel beside me. With one hand he tickled Eliza's wanton gap with such address and vigour as to cause her to shed tears of joy. With the other he pressed and fondled the somewhat relaxed pillar of my sensitive member, making as much of it as possible enter his mouth and closing his lips upon it with a most delicious suction. Beneath, I felt the lips of the wanton Maria pressed fondly against the firm cheeks of my glowing buttocks, while her fingers tickled and played with the soft slippery balls which dangled down before her.

The effect of this voluptuous excitement was so great, that by the time George and Maria melted away in the sweet delirium of satisfied enjoyment, I was again in a position to renew the combat with Eliza, whose ardour, instead of being appeased, had only been still further excited by George's tantalizing substitute for my now renovated weapon.

After having acquitted myself to our mutual satisfaction in this final encounter, which, though longer, was not less sweet than any of its predecessors, I was forced reluctantly to tear myself away from their embraces, in order that I might proceed with the necessary operations to secure our safe meetings on future occasions.

George was preparing, though with equal reluctance, to accompany me, but I told him that one could now do all that was requisite and that there was no occasion to spoil his sport unnecessarily. The delighted boy, with many thanks, agreed to the proposal that he should remain where he was.

The next morning with tears of joy he thanked me for the happiness he had enjoyed and described how well he had employed his time; in proof of it exhibiting and making me feel the condition of his limp and worn-out weapon, which hung down its head in utter exhaustion; and declaring that he had spent the happiest night of his life, and that he could never hope to enjoy anything like it again.

While he was thus amusing himself, I dressed myself and proceeded to open the different locks, and take impressions in wax of them, in order that I might get keys made to fit. Although we were obliged for a few days to content ourselves with fastening the doors with the bolts, trusting that they would not be examined, I was resolved not to run the risk of any suspicion being excited by their being found open at any future period. I then carefully oiled the locks, and replaced them.

By this time it was broad daylight, and I was forced to rouse George out of the fast slumber into which fatigue and exhaustion had thrown the lovely trio.

Without disturbing our fair partners, we returned to our own rooms, where I endeavoured to obtain an hour or two of sleep to recruit myself after all my labours.

That forenoon I carried the casts of the locks to a locksmith in the neighbourhood, whose acquaintance I had made while fishing in the river and whose good will I had secured by furnishing him with some flies, by virtue of which I had managed on more than one occasion to outstrip him in the sport and thereby endanger his reputation as the acknowledged champion of the river. I easily blinded him by making mysterious allusions to the servant maids, and in a couple of days I was in possession of keys which opened all the doors between our apartments. By means of these we every night proceeded to enjoy ourselves in the arms of our charmers, and retreated in the morning, fastening all the doors behind us, so that no shadow of suspicion was ever excited.

During the ensuing month, we indulged ourselves to the utmost, and varied our amusements in every way in which our excited imaginations could devise expedients for carrying out our frolicsome sports.

Before long it was quite evident that George was most anxious to have a little variety by entering the lists with Eliza, and also that Maria was very much inclined to try the effect of the introduction of my larger machine into her narrow slit. I was not so certain whether Eliza was willing to give up her rights over me, even for the sake of a taste of the enjoyment which could be afforded by the old acquaintance of her childhood. But after I had on several occasions made her admire its beauty and the delightful effects it produced upon Maria, I thought she was sufficiently interested in it to venture upon bringing about an exchange of partners.

I therefore one day taxed George with his inclination to taste the sweets of enjoyment with the more fully developed person of Eliza. He frankly acknowledged his wish, and said that nothing but the fear that it might be disagreeable to me had prevented him from proposing it, adding that he was quite sure Maria was just as much disposed for the change as he was as she had often expressed her enthusiastic admiration of my weapon.

I assured him that he would meet with no objection on my part, especially as he was fully entitled to enjoy all the fruits of his labour, for it was he who had originated and brought about the whole affair. I told him that if he could gain Eliza's consent, which I had little doubt of his easily obtaining, the sooner his wish was carried into effect the better.

He undertook to arrange matters with Eliza, and said he thought he would be able to manage it without compromising me in case of any objection on her part.

We were in the habit of sometimes making an exchange of beds, one of us remaining in the girls' room, while the other couple repaired to one of our rooms to pass the night.

One evening George and I were out at dinner at a residence in the neighbourhood, and did not return till after the remainder of the family had retired to rest. George told me to go to bed, and that he would send me a pleasant companion. I suspected from the way he spoke that he meant mischief, but I did as I was bid, and having undressed myself, I took my place between the sheets. In a short time I heard a light step in the room. George had extinguished the candle, and the person approached the bed and slipped into it without speaking. I was at once aware that it was not my usual bedfellow, but having no objection to the exchange, I was quite willing to encourage the frolic. At the same time I thought it would add to the fun if I were merely to act the part of a passive subject of the experiment and allow my fair seducer to carry out her freak in her own way.

Appearing therefore not to be aware of the change of partners, I said that I was tired and disposed to be lazy; and that if she was inclined for any amusement that night, she must help herself to it. At the same time I stretched myself out on my back, leaving my upright priapus at full liberty to be operated upon in any manner she might think proper. My companion immediately accepted the proposal, and turning up my shirt and her own chemise, placed herself upon my belly, kissing me fondly. She then took hold of my instrument, which was beating fiercely against her warm soft belly, and applied it to her cleft, holding it in an erect position, and bearing down upon it with all her might, endeavouring to make it penetrate into the proper quarter. All her efforts however were ineffectual to make it enter the narrow channel, for though George had not found much difficulty in forcing his way where her finger had often been before, the larger dimensions of my weapon required the passage to be considerably distended before it could enter. But the little monkey was determined if possible to effect her purpose, and proceeded to put in practice a device which George had suggested to her. Creeping out of bed, she made her way to my dressing case, and taking out the cold cream, she smeared her own secret part and my member with it, and then resumed her position, and endeavoured with all her might to force the stubborn instrument into her. She so far succeeded as to get the top inserted within the lips of the cavity; but her unaided efforts were quite unavailing to ram it home. After a long series of fruitless efforts, during which I was malicious enough to give her no assistance though her wanton fingerings drove me almost frantic with pleasure, she found it quite impossible of her own accord to effect her purpose. Exhausted and disappointed, she laid her head on my bosom, and ceasing her efforts, burst into a fit of tears.

This was more than I could stand. So saying gently to her, "You seem to be very awkward about it tonight, my darling; I suppose I must come to your assistance," I threw my arms round her waist, and without disturbing the close contact of our bodies, I gently turned her over upon her back, assuming myself the position she had formerly occupied. The instant she was aware of my purpose, all her energy and desire seemed to recur in full force, and clasping me tightly in her arms, she twisted her legs round mine, so as to hold us firmly together and retain the slight advantage she had already gained of the partial introduction of my stretcher within the approaches to her seat of pleasure. When I found myself fairly established upon her, I had nothing to do but to force my way forward, which I proceeded to accomplish as effectually as possible. Notwithstanding the repeated inroads which George had already made within her territories, I found it no easy matter to effect a complete penetration. Her toying and playing with it and her endeavours to accomplish her object had excited and irritated my organ of pleasure to such a degree, that I could no longer restrain him from pouring forth his treasures, and I shot into the confined entrance a shower of boiling liquid.

On feeling the warm effusion issue from me without her being able to make a corresponding return, she uttered a low exclamation of disappointment and regret. As soon as the pleasure fit was over, I hastened to make up to her for the loss she had sustained. Assisted by the lubrication of the parts which this contretemps had effected, I no longer found the same difficulty as formerly, and I became sensible that I was fast slipping forwards and making progress in the accomplishment of the desired object. But if I was now satisfied with the state of affairs, poor Maria was no longer so; and she evidently was becoming convinced that the proceeding was to be, at first at least, a more serious undertaking than she had anticipated. Instead of as at the beginning meeting every heave and thrust I gave with a corresponding movement on her own part, she now hung back, and as I continued my victorious progress within her, she was fairly overcome with the suffering I occasioned her, and earnestly beseeched me to stop, exclaiming that I was killing her. But it was too late now for her to make any opposition. I was too far advanced and too greatly excited to think of yielding for a moment to her entreaties, nor do I believe she would have been pleased if I had done so. Replying to her expostulations as if I had only just now discovered the impositions she had played upon me, I said, "No, no, if young ladies will come and ravish young gentlemen in the dark, they must take the consequences; but don't be afraid, the work is over now."

As I spoke I gave a final thrust, which sent me up to her very vitals, and rendered any further exertions on my part, or suffering on hers, quite unnecessary. As our bodies came into perfect contact, and she felt that my instrument had penetrated her to the utmost extent, she uttered an exclamation, but whether it was of joy or sorrow I could not discover; probably it was a mixture of both, but there certainly her sorrows ended.

I gave her a little respite, and lay quite still upon her without moving until she should be perfectly recovered from the effects of the first insertion. Gorged and crammed as she was with the dainty morsel, it could not remain long in its present situation without producing its usual effect of stirring up the passions to the highest pitch. A warm kiss and a fond pressure which she gave me, as I ventured to move my weapon gently backwards and forwards in its new sheath, showed me that I might safely venture to continue my pleasing progress to the height of enjoyment. Step by step as I kept up my regular succession of thrusts, the voluptuous excitement gradually grew fiercer and fiercer within her. She clasped me to her, imprinted burning kisses on my lips, and twined her limbs around me in all the lustful frenzy of passionate desire on the verge of fruition, till the vigorous working of my furious instrument brought matters to a crisis with her. Then relaxing her hold, she muttered a few inarticulate sounds of delight, and melted away in the pleasing agonies of perfect enjoyment; in which a few more delicious thrusts made me join with equal satisfaction and delight.

After resting for a short time to recover from our fatigues, I resumed my position within her, and gave her another equally satisfactory proof of the pleasure she was to derive from her change of companions, and with a short interval, I followed up my success with a third victory, after which, she begged for a little repose, and we soon sank into sweet slumber.

In the meantime George had been equally fortunate in his enterprise. On going to the girls' room, he had found Eliza sound asleep. After sending Maria down to me, he took his place beside his slumbering companion. He watched his opportunity to turn her gently on her back, and separated her thighs. Then kneeling over her between them, he arranged his weapon directly above the darling object he desired to enter into, and letting himself suddenly fall down upon her, he by one plunge drove himself into the inmost depths of the voluptuous cavity, and in an instant arrived at the summit of his wishes. Thus suddenly aroused from her sleep, Eliza in her confusion did not at first discover the imposition, and fancying that it was I who was thus invading her sanctuary, she responded to his lascivious caresses and entered eagerly into the pleasing sport. Something however in his mode of proceeding roused her suspicions, and inserting her hand between their bellies, she grasped his instrument with her fingers and then felt the accompanying playthings. She had been too much accustomed to handle and play with both our members, not to discover the deception; but George had acquitted himself so well and, making the best use of his time, had taken such effectual means to make the most of the advantage he had gained, that the voluptuous crisis was just coming upon her as she became sensible of the true state of matters. In such a situation it was impossible for her to make any resistance, even if she had wished to do so, and George fully accomplished his object of securing not only for himself, but for her also, such a voluptuous and rapturous outburst of the fountain of delight, that it was quite out of the question for any female to be otherwise than charmed with the performance. As he refused to give up the advantageous position he had secured and maintained his place, he worked away with unabated vigour until he had produced a second delicious effusion on both sides; he had little difficulty before the conclusion, in gaining not only her pardon, but her thanks for the exchange he had thus brought about. Indeed it turned out that Eliza's only objection had been the fear of my being offended, and as soon as she was satisfied on this point, she did not hesitate to own to him that she had been quite as anxious as he was that the two old playthings of their childhood should be thus brought into mutual contact now that they were capable of affording each other so much enjoyment. And she not only permitted, but encouraged and seconded, all his libidinous endeavours to forward their mutual bliss.

As soon as daylight appeared, George insisted on Eliza going down with him to my room, to ascertain how we had been employing ourselves. I heard him coming, and tossing off the bed clothes from us, I hastily drew Maria upon me, and impaled her upon my upright stake. Though she writhed a little at its first introduction into her, there was no longer the difficulty which she had found on the previous evening. As George and Eliza approached the bed, the first thing that met their view was her lovely posteriors heaving up and down with all the extacy and delight of unsated desire, while as her thighs were stretched wide apart over me, the pillar of my staff of life appeared and disappeared again between them every time she rose and sank upon it. This sight at once removed any feeling of restraint. It was quite evident to them that we had enjoyed the change as much as they had done, and they eagerly took up their position beside us, fondling and caressing all our secret charms and encouraging us in our voluptuous exertions.

As soon as our course was run, I insisted upon their affording us the same animating sight. George, who had been quite enchanted to find that Eliza's charming and elastic cavity afforded him quite as much delight as that of Maria, soon stripped off the scanty clothing which covered them. Then, taking up his position on the lovely girl, he plunged his beautiful weapon into her delightful grotto. No sooner had it reached the bottom than the mutual and continuous movements kept up on both sides clearly proved that their previous maneuvers had been equally satisfactory to both parties, and that the pleasing conjunction they had thus again brought about was producing the most rapturous effects upon their senses. The rapidity and vigour with which their operations were conducted soon brought on the happy crisis; and with outstretched limbs and quivering muscles, they sank in the blissful swoon of perfect and unalloyed happiness.

Nothing more could be required to complete our enjoyment beyond the perfect abandonment to the most luxurious delights of voluptuous pleasure to which this mutual interchange of partners enabled us to give ourselves up without the least restraint. There was not a lascivious fancy that entered into our imaginations which was not carried into execution on the instant. Night after night we revelled in all the delicious sweets of unbounded and thoroughly gratified voluptuousness with all the zest of youth and passion, excited to the utmost by the charms of the lovely objects of our adoration, until circumstances occurred which rendered it necessary for us to admit other participators in our pleasant pastimes. I must now bring the new actors on the scene.

The Visitors to the Abbey

It is now time to bring on the stage some of the visitors to the Abbey; and I shall commence with the party, the announcement of whose visit occasioned us so much consternation, but whose actual arrival afforded us the means of so much amusement by rendering necessary the removal of Eliza and Maria to the apartment to which we found such convenient means of access.

The party in question consisted of three persons: Mrs. Vickars, a very stout old lady, remarkable for nothing but her invincible propensity to fall asleep whenever she entered a carriage; Miss Vickars, her daughter, somewhat of a literary turn and fond of chess—probably the result of a confirmed lameness which prevented her from moving about; and last and least, though in my opinion the principal person in the group, Fanny Vickars, the granddaughter.

I should find it difficult to give any adequate description of Fanny. She was one of those girls who do not strike you forcibly at first sight, but who gain upon you, and in whom you discover more attractions the more you see of her and the better you become acquainted with her.

Her features were regular and pleasing; her form, though not on a large scale, was admirably proportioned; and there was a quiet grace about her every motion which was extremely seducing. Her whole demeanour was so soft and gentle, that one never suspected the latent fire of passion which was hidden beneath it. Indeed, we were all taken in at first and were somewhat afraid of her. I was the first to suspect the truth, and had there been no counter attraction in the way I should probably have much sooner come to an understanding with her, but I was so much occupied with Eliza and Maria, who certainly gave us enough to do, that I was less disposed than I might otherwise have been to press matters with her. Besides, she slept in her aunt's room and was so constantly in attendance upon her, and her grandmother, that there would have been great difficulty in carrying on any intercourse with her, to say nothing of the jealousy which such a proceeding might have created with the other girls. A simple event, however, produced an impression in my favour which gradually led to pleasing results.

Owing to the infirmities of Mrs. and Miss Vickars, the one from her great corpulency and the other from her lameness, they were prevented from taking almost any exercise except in a carriage, and they were in the habit of driving out almost every day. As Mrs. Vickars invariably fell asleep before she had been in the carriage many minutes, and as Miss Vickars found it very dull work to sit so long by herself, Fanny always accompanied them and played chess with, or read to her aunt, in order to pass the time.

One day the old ladies had announced that they were not to drive out, and the girls had arranged that Fanny should accompany them on their ride, and make use of Maria's pony, who being a good horsewoman was to ride my horse. Fanny had said nothing of this arrangement to her relatives, wishing that one of the girls should mention it, which they had omitted to do.

In the course of the forenoon the old ladies changed

their intention, and told Fanny to order the carriage and get ready to accompany them. I happened to be in the room at the time and saw Fanny's disappointment. However, she said nothing of the arrangement with the girls and went off to do as she had been told.

As soon as she was gone, I said that I was afraid the girls would be sadly disappointed at the change of plans, and mentioned what they had proposed to do, adding that if they could spare Fanny for that day, I should be very happy to take her place and accompany them on their drive.

To do the old people justice, they were not at all disposed to treat Fanny harshly, but they had been so long accustomed to have all their wants humoured by her that it never occurred to them that her ideas of amusement and pleasure might not correspond with theirs. On this occasion they at once gave their consent that she should accompany the girls, and wished me also to join the party. However, I was rather desirous to get upon good terms with the old people, and insisted upon going with them. As I expected, Miss Vickars and I were left to a solitary tête-à-tête, the old lady falling fast asleep a few minutes after we started; and I gained her good graces by losing, apparently with difficulty, a couple of games at chess.

We usually had a dance in the evening, and that night Fanny took an opportunity of thanking me in very warm terms for the kindness I had shown her, and expressed how much gratification she had enjoyed from her ride. We happened to be walking in the passage, refreshing ourselves with the cool air after our waltz, and my hand had not left its position round her waist. I was struck with the warmth with which she spoke, and I involuntarily drew her to me and pressed my lips to her cheek, saying how delighted I was at having been able to afford her any pleasure. There was no one beside us at the time, and rather to my surprise, she made no attempt to escape from my embrace.

Emboldened by this, I ventured to transfer my lips to her mouth, and was charmed to find an answering pressure and a response to the warm kisses I imprinted upon it. Some one approaching us at that moment, I was obliged to desist, but as she reverted to the subject, apparently for the purpose of covering her confusion, I rather added to it by whispering that I should be amply repaid for anything I could do for her by such a reward as I had just received.

My interference on this occasion proved useful in breaking the thraldom to which she had till now been subjected, and after this she was not always expected to be in attendance upon the old people and her wishes were occasionally consulted in their arrangements. Sometimes, too, one of the girls, or George or I, would volunteer to take her place during the daily drives, while she accompanied us on our rides.

In this manner our intimacy gradually increased. I could not be thus daily brought into contact with her without getting a better insight into her feelings, and I began to suspect that the occasional caresses I sometimes found an opportunity of bestowing upon her, either during our evening amusements, or when assisting her to mount or dismount from her pony were not at all disagreeable to her, and might perhaps with safety be pushed further, if a favourable opportunity should offer.

For some time, however, this did not occur, and I was unwilling to run any risk of disturbing the pleasant arrangements of our charming party of four, by hazarding any proceedings which might excite suspicion in any quarter. I therefore restricted myself to an occasional repetition of the first caresses, sometimes accompanied with a gentle pressure of her swelling bosom, or of her voluptuous, finely formed thighs.

While I was thus daily becoming more and more desirous of bringing matters to a crisis, other events occurred which rendered it most desirable that I should be enabled to insure a favourable termination to my wishes without longer delay. We learned that Mrs. and Miss Vickars were soon to leave the Abbey for a time, in order to pay a visit to some other friends and, as it was not convenient that Fanny should accompany them there, it was proposed that she should remain at the Abbey.

Other visitors were expected to come in their place, who were to occupy the rooms presently inhabited by Fanny and her aunt, and Mrs. Vivian had talked of putting Fanny into the empty room in the tower, adjoining the one which was made use of by Eliza and Maria.

This proposal threatened to disturb all our pleasant arrangements, and though it might be possible for us to continue our nightly meetings by giving Fanny the outer room, and making the girls occupy the inner one, still we could hardly hope to carry on our intercourse as formerly without her becoming aware of the state of matters. Besides this, we expected our young friend, Hamilton, to spend a few weeks with us, and it occurred to me that it would be very desirable if we could secure the co-operation of Fanny, and induce her, in conjunction with him, to join us in our voluptuous orgies.

While thus in a state of doubt and indecision, not knowing how to bring about what I desired, an event occurred which suggested a mode of accomplishing it. One morning George was required by his grandmother for some purpose or other, and having nothing better to do, I threw myself on a sofa in the parlour, where I very soon became interested in perusing the proceedings of a celebrated divorce case, which was fully reported in the columns of *The Times*. Eliza was seated at the table, with her back to me, drawing, and Fanny was sitting at the window on the opposite side of the room, engaged with some worsted work. While turning over the page of the paper, my eye caught the sight of Fanny reflected in a large mirror over the mantelpiece.

She was sitting motionless with her work in her hand, but with her eyes intently fixed upon me, and her face glowing like scarlet. I had very little doubt as to what had attracted her attention and caused her agitation.

I was quite aware that the exciting nature of the details of the case I was reading had roused up the little gentleman, who is the *primum mobile* in such affairs, and without whose interference and wicked pranks there would be no necessity for the employment of the gentlemen of the long robes and the whole machinery of the divorce court, but as there was no one in the room except Eliza and Fanny, I had not thought it at all necessary to put any restraint upon myself, or to attempt to conceal the little rogue's excited motions. I could not but be convinced that it was the manner in which the unruly member throbbed and attempted to raise up his head under my somewhat loose and thin trousers, which had attracted her attention, and which seemed almost to have paralysed her.

The idea instantly occurred to me of trying how far I could work upon her, and to what extent I could excite her passions, by giving her as if accidentally a somewhat better idea of the nature of the object which had evidently roused her curiosity. My face was entirely hidden from her by the newspaper, and as her back was turned to the mirror, she could have no idea that I was watching her in it. I therefore gradually changed my position slightly so as to enable me to present the object more favourably to her, and putting down my hand, as if accidentally, I arranged my trousers so as to give her a fair idea of the size and form of the article beneath them, which became still more inflamed and agitated by the very idea that it was under her inspection.

The effect of this seemed to redouble her interest and attention. Her eyes remained fixed upon it, and she drew back her head a little behind the curtain, so as to conceal her face from Eliza, if she should happen to look up.

This convinced me my stratagem was succeeding, and I determined to proceed still further. Moving myself about as if uneasy in my position, I tried as far as possible to exhibit the excited weapon, so as to develop its form and shape. Finding that her ardent gaze still continued to dwell upon it, I covered it with the newspaper, and putting my hand down, I unloosened the front buttons of my trousers and removed the swollen pillar from its position upon my thigh, making it stand up erect along my belly. Then tucking up my shirt, in order to give it free exit, I arranged my trousers, so as to conceal the fact that they were unbuttoned, and withdrew the newspaper. When she saw me move, she cast her eyes down upon her work, but as soon as I again took up the paper, her glance was again turned towards the object that seemed to have captivated her. I could plainly see an expression of disappointment when she noticed that the object no longer appeared where she had formerly observed it. This expression, however, soon disappeared when, pressing myself gradually forward, I made the naked head of my member slightly show itself through my trousers. The moment she caught sight of the ruby point, her neck and face became suffused with a still more brilliant colour, but after a hasty glance, she almost instantly withdrew her eyes and turned them to her work.

I thought she seemed to doubt for a moment whether the change of position was not premeditated on my part. However on finding that I continued quietly to peruse the paper, without seeming to be conscious of the exhibition I was making, she appeared to take courage and again renewed her inspection.

I waited for a few minutes, and then slowly made the stiff member protrude further forward until one half of it was exhibited beyond my trousers.

She continued to gaze on it as if fascinated with the sight of the charming object. I was just hesitating what further to do, and was trying to discover by what means I could manage to indulge her with a sight of the whole of the inflamed weapon without alarming her, when I heard steps in the lobby and a hand was laid on the door handle.

There was no time to be lost. It would not do to run the risk of being caught in such a situation, but I was determined not to lose the advantage I had gained and I resolved to show Fanny that I was perfectly aware of what she had been about, and of the interest she had taken in the object she had been surveying. I therefore dropped the newspaper so suddenly that she had not time to change her position or to withdraw her eyes, and they encountered mine fixed upon her.

The smile on my countenance made her aware of the trick I had played her. Covering her face with her hands, and letting her work fall, she burst into tears and hurried from the room. I was not quite prepared for this denouement, but I thought I would only make matters worse by any attempt to console her, I therefore resumed the perusal of my newspaper, buttoning up my trousers, so as to conceal the offending object. It was Maria who entered the room. She put some question to Fanny, who passed her without giving any answer. Surprised at seeing her in tears, Maria inquired of us what we had been doing to her to set her crying.

"Crying!" said Eliza. "Impossible; nobody has moved or spoken a word for the last quarter of an hour. It has been quite a Quaker's meeting."

But as Maria persisted, Eliza got up and followed Fanny to see what was the matter. Maria was not satisfied, and her quick eye catching a glimpse of the excited condition of my member, she at once suspected that Fanny's distress had some connection with its present condition, and said she was strongly of the opinion that I had been playing some tricks upon her. I, of course, denied this, and appealed to Eliza, who had returned without seeing Fanny, as she had taken refuge in her aunt's room, where she did not like to follow her.

Eliza confirmed my statement; but Maria, taking hold of my electric rod and convincing herself of the state in which it was, persisted in declaring that it must have had some share in the matter. I said it must have been by some secret sympathy then, for the width of the room had been between us all the morning, and told her to read the newspaper where she would soon find an explanation of the cause of my excitement.

A few minutes sufficed to rouse her passions to an equal pitch with my own, and pulling out my weapon, she proceeded to caress it in a manner that proved she was determined to allay the irritation under which it laboured. I remonstrated, faintly I must own, for her caresses were anything but disagreeable, on the imprudence she was committing; but she still persisted, and she did not desist till Eliza interfered on seeing her raise up her petticoats, and seat herself upon me, with the evident intention of inserting the weapon in its proper sheath.

Eliza pointed out the folly of needlessly running such a risk of discovery, when she had such full opportunity of indulging herself at night. Maria was most unwillingly convinced of the necessity of deferring her enjoyment, but she vowed that if Eliza treated me so ill as to allow me to remain in such a state of excitement, she would take me under her own charge, when she would make certain that I should not be able to play such tricks again during the day.

We saw nothing of Fanny till she made her appearance with her aunt at lunch. Maria rather wickedly began to rally her, talking of electric rods, metallic tractors, secret sympathies, and employing all the jargon of the mesmerists. Fanny was sadly confused, and cast a reproachful look upon me, thinking that we had joined in a plot against her.

I could not resist the mute appeal and came to her assistance, turning the tables upon Maria, so that she had quite enough to do to defend herself. For this I was rewarded with a look from Fanny, which showed that she appreciated my motive.

In the evening Fanny sat down to the piano, and George and I waltzed with the girls. Under the pretext that the room was too warm, I opened the door and extended our course to the adjoining corridor. After a while I asked Eliza to relieve Fanny at the piano, and I made her waltz with me. I took her two or three times up and down the corridor, and then stopped at the extreme end where we were quite out of sight of the rest of the party. Retaining my hold of her hand, I placed it upon my member, which was standing stiffly erect along my thigh as she had seen it in the morning. She struggled and tried to remove her hand, but I retained it, saying "Fanny, my darling, you surely can't have any objection to becoming better acquainted with the little plaything which amused you so much this morning."

She was so confused that she was unable to reply to me, and when I pressed my lips to her mouth she abandoned her hand to me and let me do with it as I liked. I made her bring my weapon up to an erect position along my belly and, opening a few buttons, introduced her hand within my trousers enabling her to have a better idea of the true nature of the organ of pleasure.

As she now made no objection to holding it in her hand and even began to caress it, I was in the act of raising my shirt to allow her to enjoy the pleasant feeling of the naked flesh, when we heard Eliza calling to her, saying that she was wanted and that Fanny must come and take her place at the piano. There was no alternative but to button up my trousers and gallop back to the drawing room, leaving her further enlightenment to be accomplished at a more convenient opportunity.

It was some days, however, before I could discover one that gave any promise of success.

There was to be an archery party given by a gentleman who resided at the distance of about twelve miles from us, and I fancied that in the course of the day I might find some opportunity of detaching Fanny from the rest of the company and accomplishing my object.

Owing to the presence of other visitors, none of the old ladies of the Abbey were able to go; but Mrs. and Miss Vickars were to accompany the young people. Fanny was allowed to go with us in the Abbey carriage, which could be thrown open, and Mrs. and Miss Vickars went in their own chaise; but I heard Mrs. Vickars say to her daughter that she had better arrange to return at night in the Abbey carriage and send Fanny with her. This hint was not lost upon me, and failing all other means I devised a scheme founded upon it.

Despite all my efforts I was unable to make any progress with Fanny all day, beyond giving her a few slight caresses which only tended to inflame and increase my ardour, and I have no doubt they had pretty much the same effect upon her. She either did not or would not understand the hints I gave her to induce her to separate herself from her companions and give me the opportunity I so longed for, and without attracting observation, I was unable to press her.

There was to be a dance in the evening and we prevailed upon the old ladies to remain for it, so that it was quite dark when we started to return home. In the course of the evening I pressed Fanny to drink a few glasses of wine to prepare her for the scene I anticipated; but she would only take a single glass, until shortly before we set out, when she asked me to bring a glass of water. I said it was not good for her to drink cold water while she was overheated, but offered to get what I was drinking myself, a tumbler of soda water with a glass of champagne in it, which she agreed to take. I however reversed the prescription and brought her a tumbler of champagne with a glass of soda water. She drank off about half of it without discovering the deceit, and then laid it down, saying it was too strong. I said that anything she had tasted was too precious to be wasted and finished the tumbler.

In the course of the evening I took an opportunity of saying to Mrs. Vickars, that as we should have to return in the dark, she might perhaps like to be accompanied by a gentleman, and that if she wished it, I would take the seat on the box beside the coachman. She said she would be very glad to have my escort; but that there was no occasion for my going outside as there was only to be herself and Fanny in the chaise, and there was plenty of room for me.

This was exactly what I wanted, and accordingly I most willingly agreed to her suggestion. Our carriage came first to the door, I handed Mrs. Vickars in, then Fanny, and jumped in myself. It was one of those roomy old-fashioned chaises which could hold three people; but as the old lady was rather of an unusual size, a third seat, projecting forward, had been inserted for Fanny in the middle, which could be raised up or lowered down as required, and which consequently formed a sort of separation between the parties in the two corners.

Fanny had placed herself on this seat, but as it did not suit my purpose that she should remain there, I, without saying a word, removed her to the corner, and took her place. The night had become stormy and wet, and I enveloped Mrs. V. in a large cloak, ostensibly to protect her from the cold, but in reality to muffle her up and separate her as much as possible from us. Under the same pretext I threw a scarf over Fanny and myself, contriving at the same time to get our knees interlaced together, so as to have one of my legs between hers.

To keep up appearances, I began a conversation with

the old lady, which I was convinced would not last long on her part. Under the cover of this, I soon got possession of Fanny's hand, and after some little toying, to divert her attention from my object, I placed it on my thigh, and again made her feel the stiff object which she had previously seen and felt. She resisted a little at first, but I persevered and, as curiosity, or perhaps desire, seemed in the end to prevail, I was convinced I might safely proceed further.

Having thus broken the ice, I removed her hand, and taking off her glove, pressed it to my lips, and threw one arm around her waist, so as to bring her close to me, while with the other hand I unbuttoned my trousers, and throwing them completely open, laid bare my organ of manhood with the adjacent part of my belly and thighs. Then suddenly bringing down her hand, I made her grasp the stiff naked pillar. This proceeding took her quite by surprise, and she allowed her hand to remain encircling the throbbing object for a few seconds, during which I felt a peculiar sort of tremor pass through her frame. But presently, recollecting herself, she attempted to withdraw her hand and remove herself from my embrace. She was, however, so shut up in the corner of the carriage that she was unable to get away from me and I managed to retain hold of her hand, and soon made it resume its position, closing her fingers round the symbol of manhood. Finding that she could not help herself, she ceased to struggle, and in a few minutes she not only made no attempt to withdraw her hand, but even allowed me to make it wander over all the adjacent parts, which I thought were likely to excite her curiosity and afford her pleasure to touch.

Having succeeded so far, I considered it advisable to

make a diversion to distract her attention from the main object of which I wished to gain possession. I had ascertained that her dress, which had been changed to a low-breasted one for the dancing party, was fastened by buttons behind. I contrived to unloosen two of them, which made the part in front open out and fall down, so as fully to disclose the two voluptuous globes of firm, springy flesh which adorned her bosom. My hand and lips took instant possession of them and revelled in the thorough enjoyment of all their beauties. She moved about uneasily at first under this new attack, but when I slipped one of her nipples into my mouth, and began to suck it, she allowed her head to sink back and left me at liberty to pursue my amorous propensities as I thought fit.

I was perfectly certain now, from the convulsive manner in which her fingers occasionally closed around the staff of life, that her passions had become sufficiently excited and I thought I might venture on an attack in the proper quarter. Stooping down, I inserted my hand beneath her petticoat, and rapidly raised it up along her leg and thigh until it rested on the mount of pleasure. At the same time I advanced my knee between hers, so that it was impossible for her to close her legs, and bent myself over her so as to prevent her from deranging my position by her struggles. It required all my address to maintain my position and calm her first agitation. She struggled so violently at first, on finding her virgin territory thus rudely invaded, that I greatly feared she would disturb the old lady and excite her suspicions. I whispered softly to her to beware of this, adding that I would do nothing but what would give her pleasure.

The precautions I had taken prevented her from being able to offer any effectual resistance to me without making her grandmother aware of what was going on; and she probably felt that after having allowed me to go so far, she had lost the power of checking my further proceedings except at the risk of compromising herself. This, joined with the insidious effect which my voluptuous caresses must have by this time produced upon her senses, soon brought about the state of matters which I desired. Her struggles gradually became weaker, and I was at length left in full possession of the outworks.

As soon as I was satisfied of this, I felt that my object was gained, and I determined not to hurry on too rapidly to the conclusion, but to attempt to bring her by degrees to be as desirous for it as I was myself. I therefore allowed my hand to wander for some time over the soft expanse of her belly and thighs, playing with the silky tresses which surrounded the mount of pleasure and tickling and caressing the tender lips. I then gently separated them, and allowed a finger to insinuate itself a short way within the soft furrow, at the same time covering her mouth and bosom with repeated and burning kisses. When she first felt the intruding finger penetrating into the virgin sanctuary, which had never yet been invaded by the hand of another, she involuntarily drew back as if frightened and hurt.

Anxious to reassure her, I ceased to force it further in, and contented myself with moving it gently backwards and forwards between the lips. When she was somewhat reconciled to this, I sought out the little sensitive object— the titillation of which affords a girl so much pleasure. When I pressed it, she gave a start, but it was accompanied with such a peculiar pressure upon my own organ of pleasure that I felt convinced she was now sensible of the sympathetic feeling which exists between the two, and that she had already begun to experience the foretaste of the lascivious sensations I was desirous of rousing. I continued to press and tickle the little protuberance and occasionally to thrust my finger a little further into the crevice, until I felt her limbs become somewhat relaxed, and her thighs open wider mingled with some indescribable symptoms of the approach of the crisis of pleasure. I redoubled my titillations, now forcing my finger more boldly up and down the narrow entrance, until a few involuntary movements in response to my lascivious proceedings, and a long-drawn half-stifled sigh, announced the access of the voluptuous swoon. Her head sank on my shoulder, her fingers lost the grasp they had for some time firmly maintained upon my burning staff, and I felt a slight moisture oozing out and bedewing my finger as she paid the first tribute to Venus, which had been drawn from her by the hand of another.

When I was convinced the crisis was past, I withdrew my finger, and allowed her to remain quiet for a few minutes, during which I prepared both myself and her for the still more voluptuous encounter I contemplated. She was now quite passive in my hands, and allowed me to raise up her petticoats, and fasten them around her waist, so as not to interfere with the delicious contact of our bodies which I now wished to effect. At the same time I allowed my trousers to fall to my knees, and tucked up my shirt under my waistcoat, so as to be prepared for the encounter.

The conversation between Mrs. Vickars and me, which had been very languidly maintained on my part, had now entirely ceased; and the old lady was giving audible tokens that she was not in a condition to pay any attention to our proceedings. I was determined to take advantage of the opportunity to the utmost, and even if I should find myself unable to achieve the victory over the delicious maidenhead in prospect, I wished to make a beginning, by allowing the proper weapon to enter the premises in such a manner as to insure the certainty of his again being allowed to revisit them on any more favourable opportunity. I was, however, at a loss at first how to accomplish this. I was afraid to leave my seat and get upon her, for fear the old lady might suddenly awake and miss me from her side, and I was equally afraid of taking Fanny on my knee.

At length I determined on the following plan: I made her place herself on her left side, bringing her body so far forward that her hip rested on the edge of the cushion of the seat, thus presenting her bottom to me, which, as her clothes were turned up round her waist, was of course quite bare. I placed myself also on my left side, and brought my belly in delicious contact with her charming soft buttocks. The feeling this produced was so exquisite that I was almost maddened; and it was with the greatest difficulty that, when I found my weapon nestling between the two delicious soft mounts of naked flesh, I could maintain sufficient command over myself to proceed with the moderation necessary to prevent discovery. I then raised up her right leg and inserted my own right leg between her thighs, at the same time drawing her to me, so as to bring the lower part of my belly as far forward between her legs as possible. Then shifting the position of my weapon from its resting place between her lovely buttocks, I lowered my body a little, till I could move forward the champion between her thighs, so that, on my raising myself up again, it reared its proud crest upwards along her belly, rubbing against the soft smooth flesh, almost up to her navel. I remained in this charming position for a few minutes, till she got over the alarm occasioned by the first contact of our naked bodies; and till I had quite satisfied myself that my position was such that I should have no difficulty in effecting the object I had in view.

When I thought she was sufficiently prepared, I lowered the point of the weapon till I brought it to nestle between the soft ringlets which adorned the mouth of the entrance to the grotto of pleasure. Then gently inserting my finger, I distended the lips as far as possible, and pressed the head of my champion forwards against the narrow slit with so much impetuosity that tight as it was, I felt the lips distend, and the point of the weapon penetrate within, until the head was wholly enclosed within the narrow precincts. I found, however, that I was proceeding too rapidly. Whether from the pain or the fright at this novel proceeding, Fanny uttered a cry which she seemed unable to suppress, and put down her hand, trying to remove the intruder from the place which he had so rashly invaded. I succeeded in preventing this and in maintaining my position; but I was sadly afraid she might have awakened the old lady, and I was obliged to remain quiet and not attempt to force myself further in, until I was quite satisfied from her quiet breathing that she still slumbered. I then ventured to whisper to Fanny for heaven's sake to remain quiet, that I would take every care not to hurt her, and that she would soon enjoy the most delicious pleasure.

I presume that the pain attendant on my first entrance had now somewhat abated, for without speaking she remained quiet and made no objection to my further progress. I tried to manage matters as tenderly as possible, proceeding to improve my position by slow degrees and merely pressing gently forward, without venturing to thrust with force. By this means I succeeded in getting nearly the half of the stiff stake fairly driven into her. But this slow mode of proceeding, though absolutely necessary in the circumstances, was maddening to me. My passions were wrought up to such a pitch by the lascivious manoeuvres I had been indulging in that I hardly knew what I was about; and every moment I was on the point of giving way to the fierce stimulus which urged me on, and endeavouring by one fierce thrust to plunge myself to the bottom and complete my enjoyment. I began also to feel that the struggle could not last much longer, for excited as I was I could no longer ward off the approach of the voluptuous crisis.

I was hesitating whether to run the risk of one final effort and burst through every obstacle at all hazards, or whether to rest contented with the imperfect enjoyment which my present situation could afford us both, when my hesitation was most disagreeably brought to an end by the carriage stopping and by the sound of the coachman's voice calling to someone in the road.

There was not a moment to be lost. I hastily withdrew my palpitating weapon from its delicious abode, pulled down Fanny's clothes, and without waiting to fasten my trousers, leaned forward to the side of the carriage away from the old lady and opened the window to ascertain the cause of the stoppage.

Fortunately I had taken the precaution to put on a light overcoat, which concealed the disordered state of my under garments. It appeared that the stoppage was merely occasioned by some carriers' carts which blocked up the way. They were speedily removed, and the carriage proceeded on. But as I had feared, the circumstance woke up the old lady. I soon satisfied her that there was no cause for alarm, and then remained silent, hoping that she would before long relapse into her slumber.

It was some time, however, before her nasal organs gave us the certainty that we might proceed with our amusement in safety. As soon as we had got rid of the light from the lamps of the waggoners, I replaced Fanny in her previous position, without finding any opposition from her; but I did not venture to attempt the completion of my pleasing work, until I had the certainty that the old lady was not in a state to disturb us. In the meanwhile I played with her charms, and tickled and caressed the mount of pleasure; but I carefully refrained from again bringing on the fit of pleasure with her, as I wished to keep up her excitement and, if possible, make her participate with me in the delights of the closing scene.

At length I ventured to take up my old position, and did not find much impediment in getting my weapon within the entrance as far as I had reached previously. Having attained this point, however, I found the greatest difficulty in proceeding further. Every effort I made, evidently occasioned her the greatest pain; and though she strove to bear it patiently, I dreaded the consequences of her doing anything to arouse her grandmother's suspicions.

While I was still endeavouring by gentle means to accomplish my object, the excitement and the ardour of my pent-up passion proved too much for me. The paroxysm of delight seized upon me and forced me to shoot into her, with the greatest enjoyment on my part, but apparently to her great astonishment, a shower of the elixir of life, which, finding no passage in front, forced its way backwards through the tightly wedged-up channel, and poured out over her thighs. She remained quite motionless, evidently surprised at the unlooked for event which had occurred, and at my consequently sinking down upon her almost without the slightest appearance of animation. It was not long, however, before I recovered myself; and as my yet unsated passions held sufficient dominion over me to maintain the original stiffness of my throbbing weapon, I still kept him in his charming quarters, hoping that the lubrication I had now given to the channel might aid his progress and facilitate his further entry.

I was just flattering myself that I was about to accomplish the complete success of my delightful task, when the carriage again stopped; and though we could hardly believe it, so rapidly had the time passed away, we found ourselves at the gate of the Abbey.

All hope of proceeding further was now at an end. We had merely time before we reached the house to wipe away the traces of my first exploit, which, as I reluctantly withdrew my still impetuous charger from his pleasant quarters, continued to pour out down her thighs, and hastily to repair the disorder in our dress. As the carriage door was opened on the side of the old lady, I had time to give Fanny a sweet kiss, and to whisper in her ear that she must allow me to take the first opportunity of completing the lesson I had been giving her, for she had merely had a slight prelude of the pleasure it would afford her. My kiss was returned in a manner which gave me every reason to suppose she was as eager for the conclusion as I was.

It was now late, and all the party at the Abbey had retired to bed. We were ushered into the parlour, where we found wine and water and some refreshments prepared for us. Fanny pleaded fatigue, and retired to her own room almost immediately, afraid lest her agitation during the previous scene should have left any traces that might be discerned. But Mrs. Vickars said that she would sit up until the carriage arrived. I told her I should remain with her, for it was no use going to bed to try to sleep as George would be sure to awaken me when he arrived.

We sat for half an hour, talking over the events of the day, until the old lady began to get alarmed at the non-arrival of the other party. I laughed at her fears at first, but as time wore on, I began to think some accident must have occurred, and at last I said that I would take my horse and ride back for a few miles to ascertain what had become of them. She urged me to take the carriage, but I said the horses had had a hard day's work, and that it was a pity to take them out again, unless it was absolutely necessary, but that I would tell the men not to go to bed and to be ready to start if they should be required. I went to the stable and had my horse saddled, and led it quietly out to the turf of the park and then set off at a good speed. I had only gone a mile or two from the park gate when I heard the sound of horses' feet approaching. I drew up, thinking that I would probably ascertain from the rider if any accident had occurred on the road.

He turned out to be a stable boy who had been sent from the place where we had spent the day to announce that our friends would not be able to reach home that night. It appeared that in passing the lodge, the coachman, who had probably been participating too freely in the hospitality of our friends, had run the carriage against a post, and although no one had suffered any injury, one of the wheels had been so much damaged that the carriage was unable to proceed. The ladies had been obliged to walk back to the house, and had got drenched in the rain, so that even if there had been another carriage at hand, which there was not, they could not have travelled in comfort. It had therefore been arranged that they should remain where they were for the night, and the messenger had been dispatched to prevent our being uneasy and to carry back some necessary change of dress, which would be required for them next morning.

I immediately turned my horse's head, and desiring the boy to follow me, returned to the Abbey. As I cantered up the avenue, my thoughts were naturally turned upon the scene which had occurred in the carriage, and the severe disappointment I had sustained in being unable to bring it to a satisfactory conclusion, and I began to consider in what manner I might still contrive to accomplish this.

After two or three schemes had passed through my mind, it occurred to me that I might not again find a combination of circumstances presenting so favourable an opportunity as was then afforded. Her aunt being absent, Fanny would pass the night alone, and George and the girls being also away, there was nothing to prevent me from spending it with her and completing the task I had only half accomplished. I made up my mind at least to make the attempt.

When I reached the house, the old lady's fears were soon allayed. The housekeeper, whom I found sitting with her, said she would get the things which were required for the young ladies without disturbing anyone in the house, and Mrs. Vickars said she would go to Fanny's room to get what was wanted for her daughter.

I wished to make certain that she was not to remain for the night with Fanny, and I said I would get a clean shirt for George and bring a carpet bag to put all the things in. When Mrs. Vickars returned I said I hoped Fanny had not been alarmed at her aunt's absence.

She replied, "Oh, no"; that she had found her fast asleep, and not wishing to disturb her, had merely left a note on the table, mentioning what had occurred that she might find it when she awoke in the morning. This information was a great relief to me, for I had feared the possibility of some change of arrangements for the night, or that Fanny, finding she was to be left alone, might bolt the door of the room and prevent me from gaining access to her.

I was not satisfied, however, until I had seen the old lady proceed to her own room, and even after the housekeeper had retired to her own domain, I watched at the door till I heard the old lady flop into bed and saw that the candle was extinguished.

Considering everything now quite safe, I hastened to my apartment, and stripped off every article of dress, putting on merely a pair of slippers and a dressing gown. Thus equipped, I cautiously made my way to Fanny's room, and softly opened the door, closing it again, and turning the key in the lock. The weather, by this time, had cleared up, and the moon was shining brightly into the room through the upper part of the window, the shutters of which had been left open. The first bed I came to was vacant, but the other presented a most delicious sight.

My movements had been so quiet that Fanny had not been disturbed, and was still fast asleep. But from her situation, it would appear that her slumber had not altogether been unbroken. She lay on her back, with one arm raised up and resting on her head. The bed clothes had been pushed down, nearly as far as her waist, disclosing the form of her bosom, and her chemise being loosely fastened hung down at one side, and gave me a perfect view of one of her lovely bubbies, with its ivory expanse tipped with the purple nipple.

I sat down on the bed beside her, and gazed for a while with delight on her budding charms. But it was impossible long to confine myself merely to their view, delicious as it was. Bending my head down, I imprinted burning kisses on her lovely mouth and exquisite breasts.

This soon roused her from her slumber, but at first she was unconscious of my presence. Moving herself uneasily, but without opening her eyes, she said, "Is that you, Aunt?"

My first idea had been to jump into bed beside her, and, before she could prevent me, get possession of her person so far as to secure the object I had in view, but I was afraid that, if suddenly awakened in this manner, she might, before recognising me, call out for assistance, and thus alarm the house. Besides, after what had passed I did not now expect any serious opposition to bring her gradually round to participate with me in all the delight I anticipated, than to attempt to snatch it from her unawares. I therefore repeated my kiss, and whispered gently, "No, dearest, it is not your aunt, but it is one who loves you a great deal better."

She started at the sound of my voice, and opened her eyes. At first she seemed scarcely to know who it was, but as soon as she recognised me, she raised herself up, and sitting erect, exclaimed, "Frank! Is it you? What is the matter? What has brought you here? Good heavens! Something dreadful must have happened! Where is my aunt?" I attempted to soothe her, telling her there was nothing to fear, and explaining the accident that had occurred to the carriage.

She would not believe for some time that I was telling her all the truth, and insisted upon reading the note, which I said her grandmother had left, asking me to light a candle that she might be able to do so.

The bed curtains were drawn back at the head of the bed, and close to it stood a large cheval glass with two wax candles on each side. I saw the good use I might put this to, and lighting one of the candles I gave the note to her to read.

While she did so, I hastily lighted the other candle, and then standing upright by the bedside, I allowed my dressing gown, my only covering, to open out fully in front, and drew it back, so as to expose the whole of the forepart of my naked person.

When Fanny had finished the perusal of the note, she raised up her eyes and the first thing they rested upon was my throbbing priapus, which the sight of her charms had roused up to a brilliant state of erection.

As soon as she caught a glimpse of it, her face and neck became suffused with crimson, and she raised her hands to cover her eyes, exclaiming, "Oh, Frank! Frank! How could you come here in such a state?"

"You should rather say, my own darling," was my reply, "how could I help coming here after what has taken place tonight, and when I found there was such a favourable opportunity of happily completing the work we were so pleasantly engaged in, and which we were obliged to leave unfinished. You cannot yet imagine half the pleasure it will give us to bring it to a successful conclusion."

It was a considerable time before I was able to soothe her, and to satisfy her that there was no risk to be apprehended from my remaining with her, for a part, at least, of the night. But I succeeded at length in convincing her that the house was closed for the night, and everyone was gone to bed. I told her besides that even in case anyone should come to her door, and wish to get admittance, I could easily escape by the window, and reach my own room without discovery.

Even after I had relieved her anxiety on this point, I had some difficulty in persuading her to let me get into bed with her. At length this was conceded on the condition that I was not to take off my dressing gown, and was only to get between the blankets, and not to get under the sheets, or meddle with anything below her bosom, which, with her mouth, was to be given up to my caresses.

It may easily be supposed that this being conceded the conditions were not long observed, or even insisted upon. My dressing gown was soon slipped off. During the caresses which I claimed the right to bestow as being within the terms of our agreement, it was very easy for me to remove the coverings which intervened between us, and without much resistance I soon brought our two naked bodies into close contact with each other.

Having now no fear of interruption, I was in no hurry to urge on the completion of my pleasing work. I wished rather by a short delay, and by making use of all the little charming excitements which are so pleasing both to give and to receive, to rouse up her passions to an equal pitch with my own, and to make her as eager as myself for the enjoyment of the coming bliss. I therefore continued for some time the prelude, by the most amorous touches and titillations which I could devise, extending them to every part of her naked body, making her in return perform the same pleasing operations on the corresponding parts of my own person.

This at first she hesitated to do, but she very soon got

warmed and excited, and without any hesitation began to put into practice every wanton trick I suggested. I saw that my object was fully attained, and that she was quite ready to co-operate with me in the crowning work. I whispered to her that I was afraid she must still have to submit to a little further pain before we could be perfectly happy, but that I would do all in my power to prevent her suffering and that she would soon be amply rewarded for what she must undergo by the supreme bliss it would enable us to attain.

I then placed her in a proper position to enable me to complete the enterprise. As I was quite aware that I had not yet effected a thorough penetration, and was afraid that there might be some sanguinary tokens of my victory, I arranged her on her back with my dressing gown underneath her, to prevent any stains reaching the sheets. Then separating her legs, and getting on my knees between them, I bent myself forward until I brought the point of the weapon to the mouth of the lovely sheath, into which I wished to plunge it.

When she saw me kneeling before her, with the palpitating weapon fully extended and standing out stiffly before me, she raised one hand to her eyes, as if ashamed to look it fairly in the face. But I seized upon the other hand and made her, not unwillingly, take hold of the extended lance, and maintain it in the proper position, while with my own fingers on each side I gently distended the lips of the cavity, so as to open up an entrance for it. Bending still further forward and leaning down upon her, I pressed the burning weapon into the fiery furnace of love, and as soon as I felt that the point had fairly gained admittance within the gates, I thrust onwards with fierce heaves of my buttocks. But the fortress was not to be gained possession of so easily. I penetrated without much difficulty as far as I had previously reached, but there I was again arrested by an obstacle that seemed almost invincible, without using a degree of force which I was anxious, if possible, to avoid. I soon found, however, that there was no alternative. The closely confined manner in which the point and upper portion of love's instrument was pent up within the narrow cavity produced such an intense irritation upon its sensitive surface that it drove me almost frantic and, combined with the excitement of my senses occasioned by the lascivious pranks we had been previously indulging in, gave me ample warning that it would be impossible long to refrain from pouring forth the blissful shower.

It would have been too bad to have been condemned a second time to waste all its fragrance on the unplucked flower, and I was determined to spare no endeavours to avoid so dire a calamity. Relaxing my efforts, therefore, for a few moments, I explained to Fanny the necessity for making a vigorous attack, and begged of her to endure it as well as she could, and to try to assist me as far as possible, assuring her that the pain would only be momentary, and would lead to exquisite bliss.

She was now almost as much excited and as eager for the fray as I was, and she readily promised to do her utmost to assist my efforts. Getting my arms round her waist, and making her cross her legs over my buttocks, so as to clasp me round the back, I withdrew the stiff member as far as I could without making it issue from its charming abode, and then with a steady, well-sustained, vigorous thrust, I sent it forward as forcibly as was within my power. I felt at once that I was accomplishing the wished for object. Everything gave way before the energetic manner in which I drove the sturdy champion forward, and I felt him every instant getting engulphed further and further within the narrow channel. This was confirmed by the delicious pressures of the lips which I felt closing round the upper part of the column in the most charming manner possible.

But if all this was delightful to me, it was far otherwise with poor Fanny. She evidently strove hard to keep her word and render me every assistance, but when I first burst through the opposing barrier, the fast hold she had hitherto maintained of me suddenly relaxed, and she uttered a piercing cry of pain. As I continued to force my way in, the pain seemed to increase, and she besought me, in piteous accents, to have compassion upon her and to desist. But I was now far too highly wrought up to be able to comply with her request, even if I had been disposed to do so, which I certainly was not for I was perfectly convinced that it would be the kindest thing I could do, to put an end to her sufferings forever by at once effecting a complete penetration.

There was no time to explain all this to her, so at the risk of appearing cruel, I persevered without any relaxation in my victorious career. Two or three more thrusts sufficed to lodge me within her to the very hilt, and I felt my belly come into delicious contact with her warm flesh, accompanied with the charming tickling sensation of her hair rubbing against me and mingling with mine.

Doubly animated by this exquisite contact, my frantic thrusts were renewed without any regard to poor Fanny's sufferings. But the feelings I endured were too delightful to be of long continuance; the pent-up tide within me could no longer be prevented from bursting forth, and with the most exquisite sensation of gratification and delight, it issued from me and found its way into her inmost cavities. Gasping and breathless with voluptuous joy, I sank down upon her bosom, no longer able even to imprint the amorous kisses on her lovely face with which I had been endeavouring to stifle her tender complaints.

After a few minutes spent in luxuriating in the blissful annihilation which follows complete fruition, I began to recover my senses a little. I was conscious that, during this period, Fanny had ceased to struggle, and was now lying motionless beneath me. I judged from this that the pain she had been suffering had by this time ceased, and I was anxious, as soon as possible, to make her participate in the delicious pleasure she had afforded me, but of which I was afraid she had as yet hardly had a taste.

The dart of love, though somewhat relaxed and diminished in size from the effects of the charming emission, still retained its position within her delightful grotto with sufficient vigour to assure me that in a short time it would be able to renew its career in the lists of love. I therefore determined to allow it to remain where it was, and thus avoid the difficulty and pain of effecting a new entrance.

Retaining my position upon her, I did all I could to soothe and calm poor Fanny. She was very much agitated, and had been sadly frightened by the impetuosity with which I had rushed on in my triumphant career without regard to the suffering she was enduring. At first she begged and prayed of me to get up, fearing that any renewal of the fierce transports I had indulged in would cause repetition of her agony.

To this, however, I would not agree, assuring her that she had no occasion to be alarmed, and that she had nothing to look forward to but transports of pleasure equal to those I had enjoyed. I soon convinced her of this, by two or three gentle thrusts of the weapon which had caused her so much discomfort, but which now, on the contrary, occasioned the most delightful sensations.

The passage having been fairly opened up and well lubricated by my first discharge, and the unruly member not being quite so fiercely distended as previously, it slipped up and down within her with the greatest of ease. Of course, at first I thrust with great caution, but I soon brought her to acknowledge that the pleasing friction it occasioned to her, so far from being disagreeable, afforded her the greatest delight; and even when our voluptuous movements produced their natural effect and stiffened and hardened the champion of love till it regained its full size and consistency, and again filled up the burning cavity till it was completely gorged and almost ready to burst, its presence within her and the fiercer and more rapid thrusts which I now allowed it to make, so far from being painful, evidently gave her intense delight. Her eyes now sparkled, and her cheeks blazed with voluptuous fires. She clasped her arms round me and drew me fondly to her bosom, while her lips returned the burning kisses which I imprinted upon her lovely mouth. Presently, no longer able to restrain herself, and losing every idea of modesty or bashfulness under the strong excitement produced by the voluptuous titillation which my inflamed organ of manhood exerted over her most sensitive parts, she twisted her legs around mine, she drew her thighs together, and contracted them closely to meet and increase the effect of every lascivious shove I gave her; she heaved her buttocks up and down in charming concert with my motions, so as to insure the most voluptuous and delicious effect from the alternate withdrawal and replacement of the weapon of love, which she took good care not to allow to escape entirely from its delightful prison. Finding her thus charmingly excited and enjoying herself to the utmost, I did all in my power to add to her bliss.

Being now a little calmer than I had been during the first fierce onslaught of her virgin charms, I was able at first to control my own movements and to direct them in such a manner as I thought would afford her the greatest enjoyment—quite satisfied that in doing so, I was only paving the way to still greater bliss for myself. I therefore watched her carefully and moderated or increased my efforts as I fancied would be most agreeable to her, until I saw from her excited gestures that the final crisis was fast approaching with her. Desirous to participate in the bliss, I then gave full vent to my own maddening passions. I heaved and thrust with impetuous fury; I strained her in my arms; and at every thrust, given with more and more force and velocity, I strove to drive myself further and further within her delicious recess.

She responded to every effort I made; her legs clasped me tighter, her bottom heaved up and down with greater velocity and stronger impetus, and the delicious contraction of the lips of her warm moist grotto closed round my excited weapon with still greater and more charming constriction. She sobbed, she panted, her bosom heaved up and down, and she clung to me as if she would incorporate her very existence with mine. Her transports were quite sufficient, without any exertion on my part, to have produced the most delicious effect upon me, and I soon felt that, notwithstanding my previous discharge, I was quite ready to co-operate with her and to enjoy in unison the impending blissful sensation of the final crisis. I had not long to wait. A few upward heaves, more rapid and impetuous than ever—one last straining of her body to mine—and then the sudden relaxation of her tight grasp, accompanied with a heavy long-drawn sigh of pleasure, announced her participation for the first time in the joys of amorous coition. I was quite ready to join her—two or three active thrusts completed my bliss, and almost before her nectar had begun to flow, my voluptuous effusion was poured into her to mingle with her tide of rapture.

I raised my head to gaze on her lovely countenance, and to watch the gradations of pleasure as they flitted across her beautiful features, while with a few gentle motions of the champion, who had occasioned us so much delight, I spun out and completed the intoxicating bliss, till at length her eyes closed, the colour forsook her cheeks, and unconscious of what was passing around her, she sank into the blissful intoxication of completed desire.

After revelling for a few delightful minutes in the thorough enjoyment of my now perfectly completed victory, I withdrew my valiant champion reeking with the bloody tokens of success, and took up my position, with my head on the pillow beside her, before she had recovered the full possession of her senses.

I was in no hurry to rouse her from the trance of rapture. Although by no means disposed to allow the opportunity to escape me without profiting further by the conquest I had obtained, I felt that after the exertion I had made, I would be all the better for a little repose before attempting fresh exploits. I therefore lay quietly by her side for some time, hardly speaking and merely occasionally pressing her to my bosom and tasting the sweets of her lips and her bosom.

But when she had thoroughly recovered from the effects of her first enjoyment, I found that Fanny was now quite alive to the bliss to be derived from our pleasing conjunction; and that there would be no difficulty on her part at least to an immediate renewal of the amorous struggle. She reciprocated the fond caresses I lavished upon her, and even indulged herself in bestowing fresh ones upon me. I soon found that her curiosity was excited by the difference she found between my person and her own, and as I was quite disposed to gratify such a natural feeling, her hands were presently wandering over those parts of my body with which she was least familiar, but which recent events had taught her were the most attractive. I could perceive her surprise, and I thought her disappointment, when, without any assistance on my part, they reached the spot where the emblem of virility is situated, and when she found in her grasp, instead of the hard, stiffly-distended object which had penetrated her, causing first so much pain and then so much pleasure by its forcible entrance, a soft, limp mass of flesh which dangled between her fingers, and which she could twist around them in every direction.

I laughed at her surprise, and told her she must not always expect to find the little gentleman in the rampant condition in which she had hitherto seen him; that his present condition was his natural one, and that it was only the power of her charms that could rouse him up to action in his fierce excited state. She was soon able to judge for herself of the truth of my statement, for her wanton caresses were already beginning to produce their usual effect upon the little hero, who speedily erected and uncovered his rosy head, and extended himself at full length, swelling out till the ivory pillar quite filled up her grasp.

She was evidently not more surprised than gratified by this sudden resuscitation, and continued to tickle and play with it till I felt that it was not only in a suitable condition to renew the assault, but even that, if much longer delayed, there was a danger of his yielding up his forces under her insidious blandishments before he was fairly ensconced in the citadel. I therefore told her that I could stand her wanton toying no longer, and that she must allow the little plaything again to take possession of the charming abode it had so recently entered, and there again offer up its adoration to her charms.

She readily agreed, though she expressed some fear lest its entrance should again cause a renewal of her sufferings. I told her there was not much fear of this, and that beyond a slight smart at the first penetration, she would in all probability find nothing but pleasure in the renewed encounter.

However, when I applied my hand to the charming spot for the purpose of separating the lips and preparing for the entrance, I found that the sanguine tide which had issued from her on my first withdrawal had now become encrusted on the curly moss which surrounded the entrance. I felt that it was quite necessary that all such traces of the conflict should be removed, and I thought that it would be more agreeable to us both that this should be done before we renewed the game of pleasure.

Turning down the bed-clothes, I proceeded to examine the spot more minutely and was somewhat shocked to find the traces of the ravages I had committed. She was a good deal frightened on seeing her thighs and the lower part of her belly covered with the crimson effusion, but I soon reassured her by explaining how it was occasioned; and the introduction of my finger within the orifice, where it could now penetrate with ease, convinced her that she had not much to fear from again admitting the somewhat larger plaything, which now throbbed under her grasp.

I was pleased to find that the precautions I had taken had prevented any marks which could induce suspicion. All that was necessary was to remove the bloody traces from our persons. This, I thought, would be best affected by means of the bidet. I accordingly made her get up and seat herself upon it. She was at first ashamed and reluctant to expose her naked person so completely to my gaze, for the candles I had lighted, reflected from the mirror, threw a brilliant light over all her secret charms; but my praises of their beauty, joined to the warm caresses I indulged in, at length reconciled her to the novel situation and she soon began to return my caresses.

Taking a sponge, I quickly removed all traces of the fierce combat, but as she seemed to be gratified by the application of the cool refreshing liquid to her heated spring of pleasure, I continued for some time to bathe the entrance to the charming grotto. She had now gained courage to take a fair survey of the wicked monster, as she called it, which had so cruelly ravaged her secret charms, and which now held up its crested head in a haughty manner, as if threatening to commit new devastations in the pleasant country he had so lately passed through. He bore, however, evident tokens of the bloody fray, and she laughingly said that I stood as much in need of the application of the purifying water as she did. I told her that as I had already performed the cleansing operation upon her, it was her turn now to do so upon me, and giving her the sponge, I sat down upon the bidet facing her, and throwing my arms round her neck, began to caress her charming bubbies.

She commenced to apply the sponge to remove the traces of the combat from my person, and was greatly amused to find the almost instantaneous effect which the sudden application of the cold water had upon the rampant object, which stood upright between my legs. In a few instants its head was lowered, and presently it dangled down, drooping its crest, and hanging over the pendulant globules, till it reached the water in the bidet.

After enjoying her amusement for a while, I told her that it was only her fair hand that could repair the mischief she had occasioned, and that she must take it between her fingers and coax it to hold up its head again. This she willingly did, and her potent charms soon effected a complete resurrection.

She had expressed so much gratification at the effect which the cooling liquid had produced in allaying the irritation of the entrance to her grotto that I proposed to her to try whether we could not manage to pump up some of the soothing fluid within its recesses. She laughed, and asked how this could be done.

I told her I would show her. I made her stand up, and seating myself properly on the bidet I made her get astride upon me, then holding the erected weapon in the proper direction I caused her to sink down upon me until it had fairly penetrated the lovely chink which was thus presented to it. When I felt that it was fully entered, I placed my hands on her buttocks on each side, and leant back so as to enable her to seat herself across the upper part of my thighs, with my weapon still penetrating her. I then told her to move herself gently up and down upon the stiff stake which empaled her, but to take care not to rise so high as to allow it to escape from its confinement.

When I had just made it enter, she winced a little, but

I believe it was more from fear than from any actual pain; but as soon as it had reached its fullest extent within her, she seemed relieved from all apprehension and willingly commenced the work of pleasure. Indeed she was so earnest in it and moved up and down so rapidly that I was obliged, in order to carry out my design, to ask her to moderate her transports. Filling the sponge with water, I introduced it between our bellies, and every time she rose up leaving my member exposed I squeezed the sponge so as to cover it with water, and then made her again sink down upon it and engulf it.

It is true that the tight-fitting nature of the sheath which thus received it, prevented much of the water from being forced up into the inner receptacle—still the pleasing coolness which was produced by the constant bathing of the heated member and which was thus in some degree transferred to her burning interior was by her account most agreeable, and certainly I found the effect upon myself equally so. The intermittent action of the hot receptacle into which it was alternately plunged prevented any bad effects from the cold application, and my unruly member, instead of being weakened by it, was rather invigorated and urged on to fresh and more strenuous action. We continued this pleasing amusement for some time till we both got too much excited and too eager for the completion of our final enjoyment to be able to endure the delay between each thrust which this proceeding occasioned.

My buttocks heaved up, and she sank down so rapidly upon the pleasure giving stake, that I was forced to abandon my occupation. At length roused to a pitch of fury, I made her throw her arms around my neck, and placing my hands under her lovely bottom I rose up carrying her along with me without dislodging my enchanted weapon from its charming abode, and making her bottom rest on the edge of the bed and twisting her legs around my loins, I thrust and drove my vigorous engine into her with the greatest energy and pleasure. She had been as much excited as I had been by our amorous play, and she now responded most willingly and satisfactorily to my lascivious pushes. A few moments of the most exquisite enjoyment followed, which every succeeding thrust brought to a higher pitch of perfection, until our senses, being taxed to the utmost degree of voluptuous pleasure which it is possible to endure, gave way and, pouring out our souls in a delicious mutual effusion, we sank down on the bed in the most extreme delight.

After this charming exploit, we both felt the necessity for some little repose, and ere long we were fast locked in slumber in each other's arms. The rays of the morning sun roused me and warned me of the necessity for taking my departure before any of the servants should get up and observe me returning to my own room.

Fanny was still fast asleep, but the view I had of her naked charms which were exposed half uncovered by the bed-clothes, rendered it absolutely impossible for me to leave her without again offering up my homage to them, and the splendid condition in which my little champion, invigorated by a few hours repose, reared up his proud crest along her belly, as she lay clasped in my arms, convinced me that he was quite prepared to do his duty. There was no time to be lost. Without waking Fanny, I lowered the head of the throbbing weapon to the spot of pleasure, and insinuated it within it as gently as possible. I met with no resistance. She made a few uneasy movements as I slowly inserted the weapon; but, overcome with the fatigues and emotion of the previous night she still slept on. I would fain have remained in my delicious quarters, and spun out my pleasure to the utmost; but time pressed, and I was forced to make the most of it. My motions became more and more excited and energetic.

At length, roused by the efforts of the pleasure-stirring instrument within her, Fanny opened her eyes, and for a moment gazed with wonder upon me.

A fond kiss and a home thrust soon brought her to herself. Without a word the kiss was returned and the thrust responded to with hearty good will. A delicious contest ensued, each striving who would first reach the goal of pleasure; and certainly, if her raptures on attaining it equalled mine, she had nothing to complain of.

We had hardly concluded the pleasing enjoyment, when a noise we heard in the house rendered it absolutely necessary I should leave her, and I fortunately reached my own apartment without being observed.

THE END